THIRTEEN DAYS GONE

A HAUNTING LOVE NOVEL
BOOK 2

AMANDA SIEGRIST

McCord Family Novel

Protecting You

Trust in Love

Deserving You

Always Kind of Love

Finding You

Dare You to Love

Mona & Mason

The Paranormal Chronicles, Volume I

Perfect For You Novel

The Wrong Brother

The Right Time

The Easy Part

The Hard Choice

Psychic Love Novel

Exploding Love

Captured Love

Slaying Love Novel

Won't Let You Go

Doomed Love

Deadly Crazy

Evidence of Sin

Finding Redemption

Obsessed Hope

Short Stories

Paint By Murder

Follow Me, Sweet Darling

Sleighville Novel

Dashing Through the Fear

Here Comes Chaos

The Last Noel

Standalone Novel

The Danger with Love

Conquering Fear Novel

CO-WRITTEN WITH JANE BLYTHE

Drowning in You

Out of the Darkness

Closing In

PROLOGUE

THE DOOR CREAKED as it swung open, making the guy behind him jump and slap a hand to his shoulder.

"Dude, this is a bad idea."

Nathan rolled his eyes at Adam. "If they didn't want anyone breaking in, they should've locked the door."

He stepped inside, not bothering to wait and see if Adam was going to be a chickenshit and bail on him. The flashlight flickered as he moved it around the kitchen. He slammed it against his palm a few times before the light evened out and remained solid.

Creakiness perforated the air again when Adam shut the door.

"I don't know what you think we'll find here. No one's lived in this place for months."

Nathan threw his hand out, smirking at him. "Look at the shit on the walls. The dude left shit behind. He might've left more he didn't realize."

"Yeah, because he killed his wife," Adam muttered under his breath.

Not quiet enough because Nathan heard him.

"Na, he didn't. The secretary did it. Jealous or some shit. His wife was banging his partner, who was also banging the secretary. She didn't like the competition. The poor old sucker just got stuck in the middle of it."

Nathan made sure to keep the light low in case someone was walking their dog or running in the neighborhood and saw it. The house might've been abandoned for months, but that didn't mean people didn't pay attention.

Nothing besides the paintings seemed of any value on the first floor. They had no need for dishes. The couch in the living room would be too hard to steal. Who wanted to buy a used couch on the streets anyway? Nobody!

He shivered at the top of the stairs as a rush of cold air swept by him. Adam's eyes bulged, then he turned to leave.

"There's something creepy about this place, man. I'm telling you, we shouldn't be here."

"Hey, you want to be a pussy, be my guest. Don't expect any of the payday when I find the good shit."

Nathan continued down the hallway to the master bedroom, snickering under his breath when he heard Adam's footsteps trailing him. That's what he thought. Adam would always voice his displeasure or concerns, but he never had the balls to walk away.

They hit the motherload in the bedroom. All the furniture was still in the room, even the dead wife's jewelry box. Apparently, the stupid, cheating bitch loved her jewelry.

Nathan laughed, staring at the jewelry box. "What did I tell you! I knew this place would have what we needed. Javier wants his money. Now we have it to pay him back."

"Good. Take the whole box. Let's get out of here."

Nathan rolled his eyes again. "Slow down, you wuss. There's more than one bedroom here. Plus, the closets."

Then he opened the lid because he wasn't about to lug the whole box with him.

"Shit!" Nathan groaned. "It's empty."

"Bummer. Now let's go."

"I'm checking the rest of the place."

They searched the remaining part of the upstairs, coming up empty. What a waste. Adam was right, though Nathan wasn't about to voice that opinion. He'd never hear the end of it.

Adam paused in the hallway as they left the last room. "Did you hear that?"

"Hear what?"

"I don't know. Like footsteps or something."

"Dude, you've been watching too many spooky shows. There's nobody here but us."

Adam shivered, rushing forward. "I'm ready to go."

Nathan nodded, then stopped in front of the master bedroom doorway. "I forgot to check the nightstand drawer. There has to be something of value in this shithole."

"I'll meet you outside." Adam disappeared from his view.

Whatever. If he found anything, he wasn't sharing it with that jackass. It was just like any other house they'd ever broken into. So what that cheating bitch died. In Nathan's opinion, she got what she deserved.

He finally hit the jackpot when he opened the drawer. Hiding in between the pages of a book was a wad of cash. That's what the husband got for not going through his cheating wife's shit! It was his lucky day. He shoved the cash into his pocket, practically skipping out of the room like he'd won the lottery. For a house that hadn't been lived in for months, it was a gold mine. Because any kind of cash, even a small amount, meant something to him.

When he reached the stairs, that same rush of cold air hit him. This time, a lot harder. Much harder.

He lost his balance, tumbling down the stairs.

The flashlight skittered across the floor, landing near the front door. The light flickered once again.

Then nothing but darkness.

1

DEALING with a dead body should be the worst thing to happen to him. But not even close. Getting a kink in his back threw his entire day off. Dead bodies were easy to deal with. He knew what to do from the moment he arrived at a crime scene to apprehending his suspect. But when an ache hit him, instead of focusing on the tasks in front of him, his mind centered on the pain. He hated being distracted by anything when he worked. Even an annoying discomfort he could've prevented.

Detective Holstrom twisted slightly to the right as he picked up the phone sitting on his desk. When it rang, it meant someone wanted to bother him, and he had things to do. One of them was definitely *not* to be bothered. He preferred to be the one to do the calling, not the other way around.

"Holstrom."

That's all he said when he answered the phone. Why add more? The person on the other end knew who they were calling. Since he was a homicide detective, they also had a specific reason for calling. There was no need to be all fancy with his greetings. He got to the point, and he expected the person on the other end to do the same.

"I got a call from downstairs," his captain started, which was never a good thing.

Downstairs meant the uniformed officer division. The cops that handled the petty shit. Things he didn't want to be hassled with. Dead bodies were his forte and he liked staying in his little box. When a call came from downstairs, it meant someone wanted to open his box further than he liked. Nothing good ever came from expanding his box. He had learned that early on in life.

"Not my problem."

"Well, Holstrom, it is now." His captain sighed, knowing he wouldn't give in easily. He never did. "It's Kade Duran's old house. Someone broke into it. Thought you might want to know."

He sat up straighter, which tweaked the already painful part of his back giving him problems today. He managed to suppress a groan because he didn't need his captain thinking he was groaning at him. Of all the calls he'd gotten from downstairs, this one he didn't mind.

That house had been on his radar since...well, since they had done that weird spell in it.

"Who took the call?"

There was a moment of silence while he assumed his captain looked for the information. "Officer Pine. Are you interested?"

"Yeah. Appreciate the heads-up."

Then he hung up before his captain could add anything else to his plate. He didn't fear being reprimanded. His captain was used to his abrupt, stern ways. So was everyone else in the department.

In the beginning, when he first started as a beat cop,

he'd been friendly, open to suggestions and help from others. As the years drew on, moving up the ladder, seeing the things he saw daily, he changed. He morphed into someone who liked to work alone, who didn't want any help, and who trusted no one. Not even his co-workers. He couldn't even pinpoint a moment in time when his attitude started to shift. It just had.

He stood up, grabbed his black wool jacket from behind his chair, and put it on gingerly. Maybe it was his mattress. Maybe it was the asshole he had to chase yesterday and tackle. Maybe it was as simple as he was getting old. But his back hurt from the moment he crawled out of bed today. Nothing he had done made it better.

But he did what he did with everything in life: he sucked it up and ignored it.

After meeting with Officer Pine and getting the lowdown on what occurred, he headed to Kade's old house. He sent a quick call to Kade himself to meet him there. No explanation, and Kade knew him well enough not to argue for one.

A neighbor had seen the front door wide open this morning. When Officer Pine arrived, the entire place was in disarray. Officer Pine had thought it prudent to contact Holstrom first instead of Kade. Holstrom had asked to be informed about anything—and he meant any kind of disturbance—with the house. He appreciated the call and that the officer had followed directions. Not everyone liked to play nice with him, especially when he had a hard time playing nice in return.

Ever since that day with the spell Kade and his weird friends had done, Holstrom had one eye on the house at all times. He didn't like the unknown. Things he couldn't see. Until he knew everything was back to normal with the house, he wasn't leaving anything to chance.

When he arrived, the front door was closed but unlocked. Forensics had been called but hadn't made it to the house yet. An unoccupied house broken into wasn't as high on the list as the armed robbery, two assaults, and one carjacking that had happened this morning. That Holstrom knew about anyway. The city had too much crime, it was hard to keep up with it all.

He let himself in, wincing at the destruction. The paintings on the walls were slashed, some even lying on the ground. The dishes in the kitchen were everywhere, broken pieces littering the floor. The upstairs showed the same level of destruction in each room.

Twenty minutes or so after touring the house, he walked back outside and waited a few more minutes before Kade pulled into the driveway.

"Detective Holstrom, it's been a while. I enjoyed the peace and quiet."

Holstrom chuckled, knowing Kade wasn't joking. He'd been on his ass every day when he'd been a suspect in his wife's murder. Kade had seemed like the perfect suspect. He'd been the last to see her alive. Too much time had lapsed between him leaving work and arriving home when he found her body that made it suspicious.

In the end, he'd been cleared, and the real killer had been apprehended. While he never apologized for his in-your-face behavior, they'd ended on decent terms. Walked away from each other with...well, not a lot of hard feelings between them. He was only doing his job, and he wasn't about to apologize for that.

"Sorry to interrupt it."

Kade nodded, yet his brows rose as if saying, "Yeah right." Then he tossed a hand at the house. "So, why are we here? Don't tell me the city is on the police's ass that I sell this place or something? Neighbors complaining? What's going on?"

"Well, someone broke into your house and destroyed everything."

Kade frowned.

"How about you take a look around and tell me if anything is missing?"

Kade nodded and followed Holstrom inside, pausing in the foyer when his gaze met the destruction. "Why would someone do this?"

"I was hoping you'd have an answer for that."

A chuckle fell past Kade's lips. "You always want answers from me that I don't have."

"You work with Detective Stewart now. Doing..." Holstrom still had a hard time accepting the things he saw a few months ago. "Odd jobs."

"Paranormal investigations." Kade gave him a shit-eating grin as if saying, "Don't be a pussy, you can say it!"

"You saw for yourself that things that go bump at night exist. Why pretend now that they don't?"

He wasn't necessarily pretending. But sometimes saying it out loud made it more real.

"Anyway, maybe someone you worked for didn't like the job you did."

Kade rolled his eyes, walking around him toward the kitchen. "Of course, it's my fault again. It never changes with you. You thought I killed my wife. Now it's my fault someone broke into my house."

Holstrom didn't know how to respond to that, so he remained silent. He did that a lot when the right words wouldn't come to mind. Most people found he was being purposely rude, refusing to respond. In essence, it was more along the lines of thinking before speaking. He'd always been that way, even as a child. Now in his late thirties, it was impossible to change a habit that had formed early on.

Kade walked through the house, slowly yet thoroughly. Shaking his head at times, groaning at other times. After venturing to every room, they convened in the foyer.

"It's hard to say if anything is gone. I left a lot here. Susana's stuff. I didn't pay complete attention to everything she brought into the marriage."

Holstrom pulled out his notebook from the inside of his jacket pocket. "Try harder to think."

Boisterous laughter filled the space. "You say that like it's going to help my memory. It's not."

Holstrom sighed. "I can't help you if you don't help me."

"I wasn't too concerned about anything in this place before I left, so I can't say that I'm that concerned it's gone. If anything is even gone." Kade sighed. "Good riddance. One less thing I have to deal with."

Holstrom pocketed his notebook. "So you don't even care that your house was broken into?"

"I want to forget this part of my life. This house is nothing but a stain on my memory. I can't sell it yet because..."

Kade looked away as his words died off. Holstrom knew the reason why. Because Mona, the weird witch, never closed whatever portal she had opened the day they tried to contact his dead wife to see who had killed her. Just thinking it sounded insane. He'd never actually voice any of it.

"Yes, when is she going to fix that little problem?"

Kade shrugged. "I don't think she knows how to yet. Every time Mason asks her about it, she says she's still working on it."

"I do hope you haven't done that..." He would not say

the word spell. He wouldn't! "That thing she did again, have you?"

"No, we haven't. Mason won't let her."

Well, that was a positive in a horrible situation.

"Now what?" Kade asked as if Holstrom had the answers. Which was so far from the truth.

"That's up to you. It's your house."

Kade looked around again, wincing. "I guess I'll get someone here to clean it up. I mean, do what you have to do, but I'm not going to stress if you don't find who did this."

Holstrom nodded, not liking the answer, but who was he to argue. It wasn't his house, his stuff.

"Why don't you have your...friend...figure out that..." Nope, he would not say the word spell, or hell, even the word witch out loud. "How to make this place safe. I think it's been long enough."

By the look Kade gave him, he agreed wholeheartedly. There was no argument on his end.

———

GROANING, she rolled her body to a sitting position. She sat a moment, twisting to and fro, working all the aches out. Sleeping on the couch was never fun, but after being up half the night, she'd given up trying to fall asleep and put a show on TV. Then promptly fell asleep. It was so annoying how that always worked out. But she refused to put a TV in her room. She'd never had one as a child, nor had her parents, and she wasn't going to start now.

The clock on the wall in the living room said she'd slept longer than she had wanted to. Ten o'clock already and she was behind in her day. Not that she had much planned, but her entire day always felt off when she got a late start.

She put the coffee pot on while she showered, changed, and applied a small amount of makeup to cover the dark rings under her eyes. Anything to portray she wasn't falling apart.

The first cup of coffee calmed her senses. The second cup had her motivated to leave the house. That was something she always needed an extra jolt for. If she let herself, she could become a recluse. But that wouldn't solve any of her problems. That solution wouldn't make her abilities disappear.

She grabbed the bright pink bag from the entryway bench, locked the door, and headed across the street to Bailey and Kade's house. While the houses around the neighborhood weren't close to each other, she had managed to make friends with at least one house on the street. The other houses, well, she'd tried once at each place, and most didn't want anything to do with her. It didn't matter how friendly she acted. It's as if they saw behind the mask she portrayed.

But Kade and Bailey...well, they accepted her with open arms because they were as odd as her.

Her smile brightened as she walked down their long driveway, admiring the Halloween decorations Bailey had put up. Skeletons and gravestones littered the driveway. As she got closer to the house, spider webs adorned the entire porch with a big, nasty-looking spider attached to one of them. A few ghosts—made from bedsheets, if she had to guess—hung from the big tree near the house. She giggled at the display, loving Bailey's imagination. Charly didn't think Kade was into Halloween as much as Bailey appeared to be.

She knocked once before Bailey swung open the door and gestured her in, but not before eyeing her critically.

"You look tired. Are you having trouble sleeping again?"

"I slept like a rock, thank you." Charly held out the bag with a cheery smile. "Also, the Halloween decorations are wonderful."

"Kade thought I went overboard, considering no one is going to see it unless they pull into our driveway, but I love looking at it all."

Charly was grateful Bailey decided to drop the sleeping subject. Sure, she'd slept great, but not until she hit the couch, and it had been a mere few hours of sleep she'd gotten. No need to go into all of that though.

Bailey worried about her too much already, and she had more important things to worry about—like her baby coming soon. She was over eight months pregnant, and the baby could come any day. Charly knew Bailey was ready for the little one to arrive. Though Bailey had told her she hoped it wasn't next week when Halloween arrived. Any day but that day. They already dealt with the paranormal enough as it was, she didn't want her baby sharing the spooky holiday.

"What's this?" Bailey asked, taking the bag, careful not to touch any part of Charly's hand.

She knew the ramifications. Charly was grateful Bailey understood how difficult it was for her to live with a curse. Because she didn't find it a gift whatsoever.

Being psychic was nothing but a headache.

The last time she'd brushed Bailey's hand while she'd been holding the envelope with the details hidden inside, she'd seen the sex of the baby before the planned gender reveal. Bailey had noticed her reaction and forced it out of her. Afterward, she had been so disappointed in herself that she hadn't waited for Kade to be there for the news as well. They'd canceled the gender reveal.

Kade hadn't been upset, but she knew it had bothered Bailey.

They were having a boy, and she only had three weeks to go until the little guy arrived into the world.

"It's just a little something. It's nothing. Don't make it into a big deal."

Bailey eyed her, as if pondering to dig deeper, then gave in, tossing out the tissue paper. Then she pulled out the bibs Charly had made this past weekend. Three total. All colorful with different designs on each one. One with airplanes. One with trucks. One with baby zoo animals. She enjoyed creating things with her hands. It reminded her she could do more than just see in the past when she touched something.

"These are beautiful. You didn't have to get us anything else. You've done so much already."

Yeah, she might've gone overboard with the gifts. But it was the first time in her life that she had true friends, and she wanted to show them how much she appreciated them in her life.

"Again, not a big deal. I won't stay long. I wanted to drop these off and see how you're feeling."

Bailey put a hand on her back as she set the bag on the couch. "Everything hurts these days. I'm ready for this little guy to come out." Then she held out her hand. "Maybe you can tell me what day so I can stop fretting over it."

Charly took a step back, chuckling. "You know that's not how my abilities work. I see things in the past when I touch things. I saw the nurse putting the baby's gender in an envelope for you, which had already occurred, so that's why I saw it when we touched that day. My visions for the future come out of nowhere. I haven't had that vision, and if I did, you were mad at yourself when I told you the sex of the baby and Kade wasn't here. You would be mad at yourself for this too."

Bailey pouted, then giggled. "You're so right. I hate it when you do that. Would you like something to drink?"

"No, that's okay."

Sometimes, when she touched things in Bailey's house, she had visions about people. They weren't always pleasant. Since Bailey and Kade worked on paranormal investigations, the things she saw would make people who had nightmares wish that's all they suffered. Because their nightmares normally turned true.

"I should go."

Bailey reached out, then stopped herself before touching her. "You just got here. Sit. Now."

Charly huffed about being told what to do, then took a seat. "Where's Kade?"

"Off with Mason helping a client. He doesn't tell me much these days because he doesn't want me following them."

"And he's right to do so. You work too hard, Bailey. It's okay to take a break."

"Says the woman who never takes a break. I know you were in your shed all weekend working too hard."

Charly wouldn't dispute it. She'd felt restless the past week. On edge. For good reason. Working out the frustration helped most of the time. Nothing would help her get past this problem she'd landed in. But it had felt good to be in her shed, creating magic with her hands. The good kind of magic. Not the kind that told a sad, somber story.

She couldn't be around people too long. Especially if they accidentally touched her. She had gotten good at how to avoid touching someone. But there were times when someone still bumped into her.

She'd never use her skill to make a quick buck. The less people who knew she was psychic, the better. But she had to make money somehow, so she built things. She'd gotten good at working with many different kinds of materials—wood, metal, fabric, yarn. Then she sold whatever she made online. The postal service picked the things up from her house. She never needed to leave if she didn't want to. She even had the grocery store deliver to her house.

"I know something has been bugging you. It's time you tell me what it is."

"I'm fine. You know I like to check in on you, make sure the pregnancy is going well."

Bailey pursed her lips as she rubbed her big belly. "Charly with a Y! You will tell me what has your panties in a twist lately or so help me..."

Charly giggled at her stern expression, not threatened in the least. Bailey would never hurt anyone, even if she could act like she wanted to.

But she meant business when she said her name in such a manner. Charly usually introduced herself as Charly with a Y. She liked people to know how it was spelled from the beginning. Some people even doubted it was her name since it was so masculine sounding.

Bailey hadn't liked her in the beginning. Charly only knew that because Bailey had confessed that when she'd been a ghost, she'd mocked Charly and how she had introduced herself. She'd apologized for her rudeness, even though Charly hadn't been aware of it. She appreciated the gesture. Now, when she said her name with the added Y, Charly knew it wasn't in a friendly way. Bailey wanted her to listen up and pay attention.

"Talk to me. That's what friends are for."

Yeah, and with what she had seen the other day...she'd need her friends more than ever. Charly averted her gaze.

This wasn't something her friends could help her with. No one could.

"Charly..."

She lifted her gaze to Bailey, soaking up the kindness and concern in them. "I went to the store the other day. You know how overloaded I can get when I venture out. I'm still trying to process everything."

Bailey eyed her critically as if she didn't believe her. It wasn't a total lie. She *had* gone into town to the hardware store for some materials she needed. But it wasn't what had been bothering her the past three days.

Charly had visions of the future. They came out of nowhere, giving her a glimpse of what was to come. They always came true. But she also saw things that had happened in the past when she touched something. Both were difficult to live with. At least when she touched something, she knew it was coming. Her visions, on the other hand, knocked her on her ass. The latest one had come while she'd been sleeping, hence the problems she'd been having sleeping at night.

"You don't have to hold back with me. I can handle whatever you throw my way."

Charly wanted to reach forward and grasp her hand, express her appreciation. She settled for a nod. "I know. You're a good friend to me."

"Best friend. Don't forget it!"

"Never." Charly stood up. "I have a lot to do today. I only wanted to drop off the gift."

Bailey stood up. "Fine. But you should come over later for supper. We'd love to have you."

Before Charly could bow out, the front door opened and Kade walked in.

"Hey, Charly. How's it going?"

"Good. I dropped off some bibs I made for the little one."

Bailey pounced before Kade could respond. "What are you doing home so early? Did something go wrong?"

Knowing the kind of cases he and Mason worked on, the question didn't need to be specific. So many things could go wrong when working with the paranormal world.

"Well, Detective Holstrom called me. Someone broke into my old house last night. Destroyed everything. I can't tell if anything is missing, which annoyed him. Nothing new there."

"That's terrible." Bailey rounded the couch, brushing her hands across Kade's cheeks before kissing him. "He'll find who did it. He's a bulldog."

Charly giggle snorted, then froze, embarrassed she let that slip. "I don't know why I laughed."

"Because laughter is good for the soul," Bailey replied with a silly grin.

For a woman who had been murdered in the 1920s, been a ghost for over a hundred years, and then miraculously turned human again, she had a very positive outlook on life. Charly envied her for that. She wished she could bottle up some of that positivity. She might portray a bubbly persona to people, but she was far from a happy person.

Then Bailey's expression turned horrified, her eyes widening. "Is it even safe to go inside? After what Mona did there..."

Ah, yes. Charly had heard about the spell to communicate with Susana's ghost. It had gone awry.

"I wasn't in there long. Holstrom knows to keep the

crime scene crew in there a minimal time. It'll be fine. I promise."

Charly saw the concern in Kade's eyes. If she could see it, then so could Bailey.

"Well, I should go. I'm sorry to hear about your house, Kade."

Kade smiled as Charly walked by them to the front door. "Appreciate it."

"Oh, you're coming later tonight for supper," Bailey insisted.

"Another time, Bailey. I started working on a chair yesterday and I want to finish it today. I'll be in my shed all day if you need me."

Bailey conceded, but she didn't look happy about it.

As Charly walked back across the street to her house, her mind wandered to Detective Holstrom. The cold, stern man who had thought Kade murdered his wife until she proved otherwise. He hadn't flinched when she said she was a psychic. He hadn't even seemed to be bothered that Bailey had turned from ghost to human or that Mona was a witch.

She didn't feel comfortable telling her friends about her latest vision. She didn't want them to worry when there was nothing they could do to change the future.

But Holstrom.

Maybe he could help.

At least find the killer to the murder she had witnessed.

2

AFTER A LONG, grueling day, Holstrom was ready to go home and veg out in front of the TV. Watch baseball or something. Do a quick workout. More stretches than lifting weights. It could help the pain in his back. Anything that didn't have to do with doom and gloom.

The crime scene crew had arrived four hours later at Kade's house, and it had been worth the wait. They found a speck of blood at the bottom of the stairs. Holstrom wasn't sure if that was a good thing or not. He'd mentioned that's where Kade's wife had been found. They had assured him the blood wasn't that old. So whoever had broken in had cut themselves. Such an odd spot to find the blood though. They dusted for prints over multiple surfaces and took pictures, but other than that, no other evidence was collected.

Kade didn't seem too concerned, so he wasn't going to be either.

All he had to do was finish a report and he could go home. Let all the open cases piling up on his desk be waiting for him tomorrow.

"Yo, Breck! There's a lady here asking for you downstairs. I was on my way up and said I'd tell you," Detective Jerry Crockman said as he walked past his desk. Then he turned, lifting his eyebrows up and down, and whistled. "She's a looker too."

Holstrom flicked him the middle finger because Crockman knew he didn't cross the line with people like that, then picked up his desk phone. "What does the woman want?"

No need to identify himself. They knew the call was coming. Why the person working the front desk didn't pick up the phone themselves and tell him wasn't a mystery. He didn't endear himself to many people. Most wanted to keep their distance and avoid him so as not to upset him. After being on the job for as long as he had, he didn't have time for bullshit. Too bad his co-workers couldn't get on board with the same attitude, maybe they'd get more done.

"She wants to report a crime but insists she only speaks to you."

His gaze glided across the paperwork in front of him, then to the clock on the wall.

6:21 PM.

He wouldn't be leaving anytime soon.

"Fine. Send her up."

He'd never turn a citizen away for wanting to report a crime. He might not be a team player or come off as the nice guy in the building, but he was damn good at his job. He liked solving crimes. He liked helping victims find closure. He liked closing more cases than anyone else. For some reason, that rubbed people the wrong way. That was one more reason why he hated dealing with some of his co-workers. They didn't care about the job as much as they should.

Holstrom flinched when he saw the woman walk into the room. He was grateful his butt was planted in the chair. Because it would've been embarrassing to fall flat on his face.

Charly with a Y.

He'd heard Bailey call her that once, and it was hard not to picture it when thinking her name.

Her full name was Charly Yarrow. He made it a point to remember people like her. The odd ones. The ones with secrets that could come to bite them in the ass. It was a fitting nickname Bailey had dubbed her, Charly with a Y. Considering her last name started with a Y as well. But he knew it was because that's how Charly also introduced herself to people. "Hi, I'm Charly with a Y."

Her blonde hair was tied back into a loose ponytail. It was nearing the end of October so the days were getting chilly, but not where people pulled all the winter gear out yet. She wore a thick winter jacket, making him think she was the type who got cold easily. The gloves gave that impression as well. Why wear gloves so soon in the year? She wore a light layer of makeup. A touch of pink eyeshadow with sheer pink lip gloss. Or lipstick. He wasn't positive which one. But her lips were shiny, which made him think lip gloss. The gorgeous tilt of her lips directed his way...

Whatever. He didn't know why he was focusing on her lips or her looks. Sure, she was a beautiful woman.

But she also claimed to be psychic. Therefore, a nut.

"Detective Holstrom. Thank you for seeing me. I'm not sure if you remember me, but I'm friends with Kade and Bailey."

He gestured at the empty chair next to his desk. "I remember you. Charly with a Y."

Her lips beamed with a bright smile as she took a seat. "You obviously heard Bailey say that. Or you heard me introduce myself to someone. No one else but Bailey calls me that. Charly is fine."

"How can I help you?"

He wanted to get straight to the point and then out of here. Forget the report he should finish. He'd do it tomorrow. Her eyes glittered with disappointment. That what, he didn't continue her odd conversation about her name? He was sorry he said her name the way he had. The day had been long, and all he wanted to do was leave. Of course, he didn't have to be rude either.

She averted her gaze, fiddling with her purse sitting in her lap before meeting his tired eyes. He wanted to see her bubbly persona from moments before. Not this sad, weary look. "Well, I assume you remember I'm psychic."

"I remember you saying that, yes."

Her lips turned even farther down into a frown, her eyes narrowing in disgust. So now she didn't want to deal with him. It was a familiar look he saw on people all the time. But he couldn't blame her for her reaction. He insinuated he didn't believe her.

He wasn't saying he didn't believe her. But it was difficult to believe stuff when he didn't witness it for himself. Her showing up that day and knocking the glass of tequila out of Kade's hand could've been a mere coincidence. Not because she foresaw him being poisoned.

"I have a crime to report."

He leaned back in his chair. "In my jurisdiction? Or in yours? Because I know you don't live in this town."

She lived across the street from Kade's new house. It was a good forty-five-minute drive for him. He'd taken the drive many times before it was proven Kade hadn't killed his wife.

"In mine."

"Then I don't know how I can help you. You need to report any crimes that occur where you live in that precinct."

She shifted on her seat, her shoulders crowding inward as if trying to ward off something he couldn't see.

"It's a delicate matter. I thought you might be able to help. But I guess I was wrong. Sorry for taking up your time."

She started to rise.

"Ms. Yarrow—"

"Don't touch me!" She flinched, backing up before his hand could make contact with her arm, pushing the chair with her.

Holstrom held up his hands. "I apologize. I only wanted to insist you stay. Is this psychic related? Is that why you're asking for my help?"

She cleared her throat, nodding.

"Please, have a seat," Holstrom commanded, glancing around the room, glaring at anyone who dared to watch what was going on. Every person he made contact with averted their gaze.

She gingerly sat down, cowering inward again. He noticed she made a point not to touch anything close to her. Not the desk or the papers lying on it. She barely even sat on the chair with her back resting against it. She was perched on the edge as if waiting to bolt. What a very odd woman.

"Go on." He pulled his notebook out of his jacket pocket, his pencil poised to take down all the information she could give him. He didn't foresee getting far because honestly, a psychic? He had a hard time believing it.

"Three days ago I had a vision. A murder."

Well, shit. Talking about crimes—that was the worst one.

"Okay. When did it happen?"

She frowned. "It hasn't happened yet."

Right. A vision. She saw things before they happened.

"Well, when does it happen then?"

"In a little over a week. On next Friday."

Today was Monday. So he had time to stop this from happening. If he chose to believe her. He jotted down the timeframe anyway.

"Do you know who the killer is?"

She shook her head. "I didn't see his face."

Moving on from that.

"How about who the victim is?"

"Oh, yes. That one is easy. I am."

He looked up from his notepad, surprised to see her looking calm and collected compared to a few moments ago when she appeared agitated and ready to flee. For someone who envisioned their own murder, she was way too calm.

"You're going to be the murder victim?"

"Yes."

He set his notepad and pencil down and leaned forward. Her chair was farther away than when she originally walked in, but she still leaned away from him.

"You're joking, right?"

"I don't joke about my visions."

"Have you ever seen your death before?"

She shivered, bothered by the question. "This would be the first time."

"And you didn't see the killer's face? How about anything else to help identify this person? Anyone you're having problems with lately? Boyfriend, perhaps?"

"I did not see the man's face. I saw his hands though,

they were white. He wore a long-sleeved black shirt. I can't give you a description of him because it's as if I saw it from his point of view, not mine. I don't have any problems with anyone. I rarely leave the house. Most things I get delivered to my house, and I never have a problem with whoever is delivering. No boyfriend or husband."

"How do you die?"

Another shiver touched her body as her gaze swept to the floor. "He...he rapes me first then strangles me with a tie. It's dark in the room, as if the power is out, but the tie is black with tiny red hearts on it."

"Ms. Yarrow—"

Holstrom made the mistake of touching her hand to offer comfort, grazing a small portion of the skin on her wrist. Because the dejected way she sat, as if her fate was already sealed, was too much to handle.

She hopped up from her seat, her eyes widening in shock. "I have to go. I don't have anything else to help you with, but I felt like I should tell someone."

Then she darted out of the room, gliding between chairs and desks with a skill that said she had perfected how not to touch anything as she moved.

Very odd woman.

Now that she ran away from him, he'd have to pursue.

Because he wasn't one to let anything slide. Even if he didn't believe her, he'd do his due diligence.

She wasn't dying on his watch.

———

CHARLY CLOSED her front door and leaned against it a moment, letting her nerves calm down. The walk out of the precinct had been tense, her body alert and ready for Detective Holstrom to stop her. Surprisingly, he didn't. The drive home was also anxiety-induced, waiting for sirens or something to follow her. Make her pull over and confess all her sins.

But she made it home with no one stopping her.

She hung her keys up on the wall near her coat rack in the corner, added her coat as well, and then tossed her purse on the bench. She tore each glove off, dropping them next to her purse. She always got odd stares wearing gloves when the weather wasn't cold enough. Right now, she was pushing it with glove season. But she chose her comfort over weird looks. When she didn't touch things or people skin-to-skin, she didn't see anything she shouldn't. While she didn't always wear gloves going out in public, it was a must at a place like a precinct where way too many people going through turmoil convened.

A shower was needed. She always felt dirty walking out of the house and venturing near people. As if their auroras would attach to her and send her into a downward spiral of visions.

The water soothed her weary bones and lifted her mood. After she dressed in a T-shirt too large for her and a pair of sweats she'd had for over five years, she decided a strong drink would settle the rest of her agitation.

The doorbell stopped her from entering the kitchen.

A glance through the peephole told her she'd made a mistake. Telling that detective about her vision hadn't been wise. How could she forget he was a damn bulldog?!

"Detective Holstrom, how can I help you?" she asked with a merry smile after opening the door.

One way to avoid people's odd stares and disapproving looks was to portray a happy-go-lucky persona. They couldn't think anything was wrong with her if she appeared bubbly and full of pleasantries. Sometimes, she even overdid it. It was also the reason she wore pink a lot. Pink was a happy color. Nobody ever frowned at the color pink.

"I didn't think our conversation was concluded. You left very abruptly. I have more questions. May I come in?"

God, no! She didn't want this man in her house. His essence would linger anywhere he stepped or sat or touched. She'd already seen something she didn't want to see about him. Something he wouldn't appreciate her knowing without him telling her.

"Ms. Yarrow, you came to me for help. Let me help you."

Her grip on the doorframe intensified. "I came to you so someone would know the details. Perhaps a head start on finding the killer. But don't think for one minute you can actually help me."

His brows puckered. "I'm a very determined man. Something I know you realized, otherwise you wouldn't have come to me. I will stop this from happening."

She shook her head, laughing with no spirit behind it. "No, you won't. No matter how hard you try, you won't."

"I will."

"You won't."

He huffed, his stance strengthening as if prepared to grab her shoulders to shake some sense into her. She'd have to slam the door in his face if he tried to touch her again.

"Look, detective, what you fail to realize is my visions always come true. Always. I've never had one not come true. So it's not that you won't stop it because of some error on your part, it's because it's already been decided. I will die."

"You saw Kade's death and stopped it."

She put up a finger. "Correction, I saw the bottle of tequila being poisoned, not his actual death. The bottle was poisoned, I didn't stop that. Which means that the vision still came true. As they always do," she emphasized.

"I won't continue to argue with you." Though the sly smirk said he was right and she would be wrong. "I would still like to come in and ask more questions. I don't have enough information yet."

Well, she could agree she was abrupt in her departure. It wouldn't hurt to let him ask a few more questions, even if she didn't want him in her domain.

"Fine. I was going to have a drink. Would you like one?"

She opened the door farther, gesturing him inside. She made sure to stand back far enough so he wouldn't touch her as he entered.

He shook his head. "I'm on duty. I can't."

Whatever. More for her.

"This way."

Then she walked away, needing that drink more than before. He took a seat at the island counter while she poured herself a glass of wine to the top. Something stronger, like the scotch hidden behind the wine bottles, would've been nice, but she needed to be level-headed with the detective in her house. Scotch always hit her harder than wine, and a lot faster.

She took a large sip. "So, what else do you need to know?"

"Everything." Then he pulled out the same notebook he had at the precinct and a pencil. "Even the slightest detail, which may seem minor to you but could be crucial to me, is important. How do you know it's next Friday?"

"That's easy. I saw the date circled. Like that." She pointed to the calendar hanging next to her fridge. Bright red circles swarmed the day.

"What's happening that day? It's the day after Halloween. I'd think you'd circle the holiday instead."

Was he dense?

"Umm...I'm dying."

He didn't look amused. "Why'd you circle the day to begin with?"

"I'm dying. I circled it after I had the vision. It wasn't circled before that, so I know I did it for a reason. That is the reason."

"You said it was dark in the room. Where were you?"

Okay. An abrupt conversation switch, but she'd go with it.

"The living room. I usually have the light on, but I also like the lamp next to the couch on. I like to read at night, and the extra light helps to see."

"Do you have a clock in the living room?"

"No."

He nodded, jotting something down on his pad. "So you can't determine a time? Unless the TV was on?"

"Completely dark, as I said."

He scribbled more in his notebook. "We know it's evening then. I'm going to guess before bedtime since you're in the living room. The lights go out. Perhaps a storm. Perhaps the person cuts the wires."

"Not necessarily before I'd go to bed. I have been sleeping on the couch for the past few days. I can't seem to fall asleep in my room."

"What are you wearing?"

She paused with the wineglass to her lips. Odd. She never processed what she had on that night. The wineglass hit the counter with a soft clink as she closed her eyes.

Her mind trailed back to the vision, venturing to every corner, eyeing every tiny detail.

Her eyes snapped open. "A pink tank top, no bra. I have on a pair of loose drawstring pants, black."

A hint of a smile touched his lips as he marked more onto his pad. "Is that what you normally wear to bed?"

She couldn't hide her own smile. "No."

He glanced up. "What do you wear then? We can determine if this is during the middle of the night or before you go to bed."

Her smile widened even more. "Nothing."

He coughed as if to cover a groan, then moved his gaze to his pad. "So it could be before bedtime as I originally said."

"I don't sleep naked on the couch."

His eyes drew to her once again.

"It could be something I threw on to fall asleep on the couch. I do have guests on occasion. I'm sure no one wants to sit where I've been lying naked."

He shifted in his seat but didn't say anything for a moment. "Of course. And you said you had no bra on, so you're right as well. Therefore, we can't pinpoint an exact time."

"I suppose not."

She chose not to tell him she had no bra on at the moment either. Why put one on when she had no intention of going anywhere? She hadn't expected him to come here tonight. She figured if he wanted more answers he would've followed her out of the precinct.

"At what point does the vision start? I assume in the kitchen if you saw the calendar on the wall."

"Yes, I'm at the sliding door." Her hand glided to point at the door to his right. "I don't know why I'm standing there. I don't make a habit of standing in front of it, not even to look out in the woods. He's stares at me for a few seconds. At my back." She wished she didn't know that detail. That she would be vulnerable like that. Knowing a killer had the upper hand from the very beginning. Shaking those thoughts loose, she continued, "I hear a noise, and as I turn, he's right in front of me."

"But you make it to the living room. How?"

Ugh. He was going to make her go through every. Single. Detail. He hadn't lied about that part. She didn't want to. She didn't want to relive a moment of it, especially when she knew she'd dream about it tonight.

More wine disappeared down her throat.

"I will have a glass with you. It's okay, Ms. Yarrow, I want you to take your time. I know this isn't easy for you."

Changing his mind about the wine surprised her. He seemed like a very by-the-book, no bullshit kind of man.

But she'd take him up on the offer because it would make her more relaxed to know they were on the same level.

She poured him a glass and refilled hers, then closed her eyes again to see each moment as it happened.

3

BRECK TOOK the glass after she pushed it his way, then lifted it to take a tiny sip. He might've changed his mind, but he still needed to be levelheaded. He'd only told her he'd have one because he hated the panic on her face. The moment he asked for the glass, a wisp of a smile appeared. She had a beautiful smile.

While he wasn't sure what to think of her so-called vision, he would take it seriously as if it were going to come true. He wouldn't have another person's death on his conscience.

"This is good. Thank you."

She nodded, then gulped more down. If he didn't get the full story out of her soon, he might not get it at all. She wasn't taking her time drinking the wine.

"The sliding door?"

"Yes, right." She cleared her throat, her eyes gliding to the spot where her story would begin. "As I said, I was standing there and I heard a noise. I turned around and he was right in front of me. He shoved me hard against the door, knocking my head, dazing me at first. But I fought back. We tussled and I grabbed the vase of flowers here," she said, her long fingers making a short gesture to the red roses sitting pretty on the counter.

"Do you always have flowers on the counter?" She'd stopped speaking, so he figured that was his cue to get her back on track.

She shook her head as if lost in thought and clearing her mind, then nodded. "Yes, I switch them all the time. Different flowers, different colors."

"Is it the roses you see?"

She looked perplexed by the question, then closed her eyes, the same as she did before when thinking back to the vision.

"No, they're pink carnations. They look fresh as if they're new." Her eyes snapped open, and she smiled. "These are details I've never thought about."

He matched her smile. "Like I said, every detail is important. What do you do once you grab the vase?"

"I smash it against his head."

A chuckle slipped out before he could stop it. "Good for you."

"Well, yes, one small victory. He still kills me." She looked resigned to the fact, more wine disappearing from her glass.

Right. Mrs. Doom and Gloom was back. If there was one trait in life he loved to display, it was proving people wrong. He'd had to showcase one too many times that annoying attribute. Well, at least annoying to others. He enjoyed immensely being right. He'd make her vision false if it was the last thing he ever did.

"What happens next?"

"I run. I make it as far as the living room where he jumps

on me from behind and we tumble to the ground. He gets the upper hand very quickly. He's strong. Once he's on top of me, I can't fight back. Not to the degree to get away. There's nothing in my reach. I fight, but he wins."

Silence fills the room.

He assumed the part she wasn't going into detail about was the part where he rapes her. He gets the upper hand so fast, she can't do anything to stop it. Breck didn't want to hear it, but he needed details. Some of them, anyway.

"Do you scratch him? Bite him? Draw blood of any kind?"

"I don't know if the vase to the head cuts him, but I do claw at him while he has me pinned down. I can't say whether I draw blood. I'm not seeing it through my eyes, remember? It's through his."

"How long from the point he starts attacking you to....the end"—he coughed, clearing his throat, hating to point out her death—"do you think it is?"

Her brows puckered as she contemplated. "I don't know. Maybe ten minutes. It feels like an eternity when it goes through my mind."

"Does the vision end when..." He tilted his head, awkwardness filling him up at the fact he couldn't say it...*when you die.*

"Once I take my last breath, yes, it ends there. I see nothing else."

"Does he say anything during any of it?"

She looked perplexed again, as she processed the question. Then her eyes widened, and she nodded.

Breck leaned forward when she didn't continue. "And?"

"As he's squeezing the tie around my neck, he leans down and whispers in my ear, 'You were right.' I can't believe I didn't remember that right away."

This time Breck was confused. "What does that mean?"

She shrugged. "I have no idea. Maybe he knows I envisioned it all."

A chill rushed up and down his spine as Charly looked as if she were lost in her own world again.

"How would he know that?"

Now Charly looked annoyed. "Again, I don't know."

"Perhaps it's someone you know. Someone you told about the vision."

A crooked grin appeared on her lips. "You're the only one I've told, so..."

So he wasn't the killer, and his question would remain unanswered.

"Why haven't you told anyone else?"

"Why would I? I don't want to worry my friends. There's nothing I can do about it. It is what it is."

He frowned, hating the finality in her voice. "It can be stopped."

"It can't."

"I'll make sure it is."

She scoffed. "Your arrogance knows no bounds."

He smirked. "Confidence. There's a difference."

"What part of my visions always come true didn't you understand?"

"There's a first time for everything, Ms. Yarrow. Don't you know that?" He held onto his glass, but he hadn't taken another sip. By the heated glare in her eyes, he felt compelled to take another one. She didn't like his insistence that she was wrong. Many people didn't when he acted that way. "What about family?"

She flinched. "Excuse me?"

"You said you didn't want to worry your friends. What about worrying your family?"

"I have no family anymore. My parents died when I was a teenager. Only child. No extended family. That I've met, anyway."

Sensing it was a topic off-limits, he didn't dig deeper. He assumed no contact with other family members was due to the psychic abilities she claimed to have.

"Have I answered all your questions?"

"The ones I have so far, yes."

She straightened, gulping more of her wine before saying, "Then I'll show you out if you have nothing else to ask."

"Eager to get rid of me? Why?"

"Because I'd like to get drunk, and I can't do that with someone else here."

Honest, yet what an odd thing to say.

"Why not?"

She rolled her eyes, either because she was annoyed by his continued questioning or by the specific question. "Because it's harder to maintain control on what not to touch when I drink. I don't want to touch you again and see —" Her eyes widened as she stopped speaking, realizing she said too much.

"First of all, I touched you in the precinct, not the other way around. And second,"—he narrowed his eyes, displaying the wrath that could arise when certain buttons were pushed—"what did you see? You had a vision when I touched you?"

"No, my visions come out of nowhere. They attack at the most horrible times sometimes. I can't prepare for them. But when I touch things or *they touch me*," she emphasized, conceding he was correct, "I see things...from the past. Things that have already happened."

Meaning she saw something in his past.

"What did you see?" he asked through gritted teeth. Part of him didn't want to know, the other part had to know.

"It wasn't your fault she died."

No one knew about that unless he wanted them to know. And damn it! He didn't want people to know.

He stood up so fast, the chair scraped against the floor with a loud screech. "I'll leave you to your evening, Ms. Yarrow. Good night."

Then Breck left before he did something he'd regret. Like lash out at a woman who had no control over her abilities.

Because he might not have believed her before, but it was hard to deny when she knew things she couldn't possibly know.

He paused before peeling out of her driveway, an uneasy feeling clenching his gut. He left abruptly. Maybe too abrupt. Someone was out there, going to kill her. Of course, they had over a week before it happened, but still.

He found his car going across the street instead of onto the road. Then his fist was knocking on a door he thought he'd never see again.

Bailey, the former ghost—still odd to think about— answered the door. "What do you want?"

Straight and to the point. He had always liked her from the moment he met her, even if she had scared the living daylights out of him.

"To speak to you and Kade about a matter that is both concerning and delicate."

She pondered his words for far longer than he liked, then waved him inside. "Kade! That *detective* is here."

By the way she said detective, with a hint of disgust, told him he wasn't endearing himself to these two, and never would.

Nothing new there.

Kade groaned when he walked into the living room. "Did you find who broke into my house already?"

"No." He doubted he would either. There wasn't much evidence to go on. "This is about something else. I don't usually break a confidence or talk about my cases with anyone else. My gut tells me I should though."

If there was one thing in life that he knew he should always follow, it was his gut. Because the last time he ignored it, a life was taken too soon.

CHARLY WHINED when loud pounding sounded on her front door. She'd consumed the glass she'd filled in front of Detective Holstrom after he left and filled it to the rim again. She was halfway finished with this new glass, and she didn't want to be interrupted by anyone else. More than likely, it was the obstinate man again. With more questions, and on a topic she should've never brought up.

"You open this door right this instant, Charly with a Y, before I break it down!"

Oh, it was Bailey. And she sounded upset.

As much as she wanted to take her time answering the door, she heard the anger mingled with desperation in her tone. When she swung the door open, she was surprised to see Kade behind her looking as concerned as Bailey.

"What's wrong?"

"You lied to me," Bailey spat as she brushed past her, though was careful not to touch her.

Charly followed her into the living room, letting Kade handle the door. So much for keeping her house free of others' essence.

Bailey paced in front of the TV. Charly decided to take a seat on her pink loveseat against the wall, waiting for Bailey to spill what she had apparently lied about. Kade stood off to the side, letting Bailey get her ire out.

"We had a visit a little bit ago. Do you want to guess who it was?"

Well, even a psychic didn't need a vision all the time to figure things out. Detective Holstrom ratted her out to her friends. So much for trusting the man.

"That wasn't his place to tell you."

"No, it wasn't!" Bailey shrieked. "You should've. I knew something was bothering you, and you told me it was nothing."

Charly slouched into the couch, downing more of the wine. "My visions always come true, Bailey. Always. I didn't want to worry you. Not when you're so close to having the baby."

"How dare—" Bailey stopped in her tirade when Kade put a hand on her shoulder, letting her know with one simple look she had to calm down. They had a connection that made Charly jealous on so many levels. Made her yearn for something she knew she'd never have. Even with impending death on the horizon.

"What Bailey is trying to say is friends trust each other with their visions, even if they think there's nothing they can do."

"You say that as if you also have visions, and we both know that's not true, Kade."

"You know what I'm saying. We can—"

"No!" Charly snapped, lunging to her feet, sloshing some of the wine. "You can't stop this. Just as Detective Holstrom couldn't get it through his thick skull, neither can you. They. Always. Come. True. I should've never told him.

This is exactly why I didn't tell you. I didn't want it to become a thing."

"Fine. So it'll come true." Bailey's lips thinned. "It doesn't mean you should go through it alone. It doesn't mean we can't try together to stop it. You've been alone a long time, Charly. I know how it feels to be alone for so long. You know I know."

Yes, spending over a hundred years in a house where no one could see or hear you was being alone for a very long time. Bailey would understand the feeling better than most people. Not that she'd been alone as long as that. More like only about twenty years.

"It doesn't mean you have to be alone anymore. We're friends. Right?"

"Yes. Of course."

"Then friends tell each other things like this. They don't go to stern, unfriendly detectives first." Kade made a sound that had Bailey pouncing on him. "Excuse me? Is there something you'd like to add?"

"I don't fault Charly for going to Holstrom. He is good at what he does. If anyone can find a killer before the actual crime occurs, it's him."

Bailey rolled her eyes, crossing her arms. "He thought you killed Susana. Doesn't exactly inspire confidence on my end."

"Yeah, but he didn't give up. He was in my face constantly. He was working the case until the end. He had Todd as a suspect, and I had no clue about that. He worked every single angle. I was just too pissed off to see that. I only saw what he wanted me to see. That man keeps a lot close to his chest."

Charly would agree with that. By his reaction to her

confessing what she'd seen when he touched her, she knew not many people knew the story.

"Whatever. Bottom line, Charly," Bailey said, pointing a sharp finger at her, "we're not leaving your side until this killer is caught."

"Bailey..."

"Non-negotiable."

Charly stared at her large belly. "You're pregnant. You shouldn't be anywhere near me."

"Agreed," Kade said before Bailey could argue with her. "That's why I called Donnie. The guys have your house covered during the night. During the day, I'll be here."

Charly groaned, plopping back down to the couch. "I don't need a bunch of vampires watching my house."

"It's like you're ready to die. Just accepting your fate. What is wrong with you?" Bailey exclaimed.

Was she? Ready to die? Accepting her fate?

Maybe she was a little.

Life wasn't easy. It hadn't been even as a child. Her parents had been loving and so supportive of her so-called gift. They thought of it as something special. She saw it as a curse. Though they never forced anything on her, she had never come to terms with her abilities. She tried to avoid them at all costs. Despite that, the visions always reared their ugly head and forced her to take action. She hated having such a good conscience.

There would be peace in death.

Because life held nothing but torment.

But arguing with Bailey was the last thing she wanted to do, especially in her condition. If anything happened to the baby and it was her fault, she'd never forgive herself. She'd hate to haunt the halls of this house after she died. Being a ghost wouldn't be fun.

"Okay. Let them come. It won't make a difference, but if it makes you feel better, then okay."

"I don't like how resigned you sound." Bailey's ire was losing its flame.

Charly's shoulders slugged up then down carelessly. "I won't keep repeating myself, so this will be the last time I say it. The visions always come true."

"I want to hug you right now."

Though Charly saw the desperation on Bailey's face, she didn't move a muscle to get closer. They both knew nothing good would come from it.

"It's going to be okay, Bailey. I promise."

Bailey huffed, crossing her arms. "Nothing is okay, and trying to make it sound like it will be doesn't change anything."

They could go 'round and 'round in circles, so Charly decided to remain silent. Bailey continued her pacing. Kade darted his gaze back and forth but didn't say a word. Not long after, Donnie and Joe arrived. Kade and Bailey left, despite Bailey's protests to stay a little longer. Thankfully, Kade ushered her out.

Charly didn't move once from the couch. She didn't even produce a fake, bubbly smile for the two handsome vampires standing in front of her.

"I'll be going to bed soon. You two can make yourself at home here. Or the kitchen. Doesn't matter. My house is yours."

Donnie inclined his head with a gentle smile. "We appreciate the offer. We'll be outside if you need us. Just say our names out loud."

Not yell. Not call. Simply say their names. Because they were vampires and had superhuman hearing.

"You don't have to be outside."

"We know." Donnie headed for the door, Joe trailing him. "You're safe, Charly. We'll make sure of it."

She nodded, then focused on her glass when they left the room. She could open another bottle and drink herself to oblivion. Or she could sober up and go to bed.

The second bottle won.

4
___

"No. Not yet." Breck groaned as he reached across the bed to his nightstand, fumbling for his ringing phone in the dark.

He didn't need to look at the screen to know it was work-related. No one else ever called him in the middle of the night.

"Holstrom."

"Dead body. I'll text you the address."

Then the officer on the other end hung up. Officer Pine. Good guy. Worked hard. He was studying to take the detective's exam, move up on the ladder. Holstrom liked him, especially because he didn't talk his ear off at three in the morning. Some did when they called. Drove him up the wall.

He rolled out of bed, quickly dressed, brushed his teeth, and grabbed a granola bar out of the pantry before leaving. Who knew when he'd get something to eat? He could've used a coffee, but there wasn't time. Duty called. His back, after stretching it out last night and popping a few pain pills, was feeling better. So there was one positive in this shitty morning.

When he pulled up to the apartment building on the west side of town, he made a note of everything. How many cop cars were there with their flashing lights. Overkill and brightly displaying "we got a crime here!" Could've used less gawkers.

How many cars were in the lot? He'd make sure one of the officers wrote down all the license plate numbers for him.

Who was hanging around, observing the chaos? Another officer would take their names and numbers for him. Why stare at the commotion at three-thirty in the morning? Why were they up so early to begin with?

He nodded at one of the officers stationed at the door and walked inside to the third floor. Another officer guarded the door to apartment 321. Officer Pine was in the living room chatting with one of the crime scene techs. Maybe he was a little slower than he realized. He always beat the crime scene crew.

"Hey, detective. She's in the back bedroom." Officer Pine waved his hand down the hallway, letting Breck take the lead.

"Who called it in?" Breck asked as he pulled out his trusty notebook.

"Boyfriend. He got in a little after two o'clock. Closed down the bar a few blocks away. She had to work early today and didn't want to join him."

If she were alive, she'd be regretting that decision right about now. Though Breck didn't say it out loud. Some liked to joke around a crime scene. Even laugh about things that weren't funny. Everyone tried to process death and mayhem in different ways. He always kept his thoughts to himself.

"Coroner here yet?"

"On his way."

Breck paused outside the bedroom. "What do you think about the boyfriend?"

"Drunk. Quiet. Can't tell if that's because he's still in shock finding her or if he did the deed himself." Officer Pine shivered as he continued. "Her body's still warm. She hasn't been dead long."

Interesting. Perhaps an open-and-shut case. Idiot was so drunk he killed her then called the cops on himself.

He stepped inside the room, his heart stopping in its tracks.

The woman, young twenties, was sprawled across the middle of the bed, naked. Bruises marred her wrists, and the damage below said whoever had held her down hadn't been gentle when they raped her.

But it was the dark-blue tie wrapped around her neck that had his skin crawling with terror.

Charly's vision was coming to life. Wrong victim, but same picture.

"Anyone hear screams? Noise? Something?"

Officer Pine shook his head, whispering as if afraid to disturb her, like she was only sleeping or something. "Only call to nine-one-one was the boyfriend. We haven't started knocking on doors yet. The neighbor across the hall opened the door and asked questions, but they also reported they didn't hear anything odd."

"Forced entry anywhere?"

"Not that I could see."

Breck appreciated the fact that every time he asked a question, Pine had an answer. Competent and thorough. He'd pass the exam and make a great detective.

"I want to speak to the boyfriend."

"He's outside in a cruiser."

Breck found the man and didn't spend much time questioning him. His eyes were glossy and unfocused. His words slurred. He was so drunk, Breck didn't think the man touched a hair on his girlfriend. He didn't have the coordination to kill her. When he sobered up, he'd drill the man about every second of his evening.

Waking up everyone on the floor wasn't pleasant, but it had to be done. When he finished the third floor, he made his way down each level. Nobody had heard a thing. The coroner relayed he was estimating the time of death between one and two o'clock. So if the boyfriend didn't do it, which Breck believed, then he could've missed the killer by minutes.

So that begged the question, was it random? The killer got lucky not getting caught. Was it planned? They had known the boyfriend wouldn't be there?

Breck drove to her work, a coffee shop in the downtown area. Good thing, because he needed a cup of java. He ordered one before asking to speak to the manager where he then relayed the terrible news. It took a while for the woman to calm down and find her voice before she was able to answer his questions.

Carla Thompson, age twenty-two, had been working at the place for the past three months, trying to survive while she applied for positions in the accounting world. She had a degree in finance but found it difficult to get her foot in the door anywhere. She was a decent employee. Showed up on time, worked with a smile, and didn't complain about anyone—co-worker or customer.

He interviewed her co-workers next. All said the same thing. They even had nice things to say about the boyfriend, besides the part where he liked to drink too much. Though they all agreed he didn't have a temper. Just no self-control on drinking. Breck still didn't believe the man killed his girlfriend. But it didn't mean the man was off the suspect list. The time of death was too close to when he arrived home, so his alibi wasn't rock solid. Anyone could turn on a dime.

By two o'clock in the afternoon, his stomach finally hollered it was time to eat. He grabbed a burger from a fast-food joint, then hit the road. To the last place he wanted to go. Especially with the way he abruptly left yesterday.

He knocked on the door with a solid thump, though he wasn't feeling as confident as he would like. He'd wanted her vision to be nothing but nonsense. Now it had turned into reality.

Breck jerked when Kade opened the door, not expecting him, which was silly. Because he'd told those two last night about Charly's vision. Of course, they'd take her safety seriously. Well, good. Because she needed protection now more than ever.

"Holstrom. You look like shit."

And he felt like it.

"I need to speak to Charly."

Kade waved him in, pointing toward the kitchen. "She's back there. Be gentle with her. Don't be a hardass. She doesn't deserve that."

Breck didn't take his warning personal. He knew how Kade saw him. How most people did. He wouldn't dispute the hardass trait at all. He was one.

But Kade was right. None of this would be easy, and he didn't want to hurt her in any way.

Though he wasn't about to tell Kade any of that. What he said or did concerning Charly was none of his business.

He walked away, chuckling when he heard Kade swear under his breath what a jackass he was.

Charly was bustling around the kitchen. The counter was filled with enough ingredients that it was hard to pinpoint exactly what she was making. She jumped, exclaiming loudly when she noticed him.

"Detective, what a surprise! You're back so soon."

Breck slid onto a chair, trying for a light smile. One that said he was here as a friend, not a detective. If he wanted to work with her to solve her future murder, the death on his hands today, he needed her to be at ease with him. Not on her guard. Not constantly watching what she said to him.

"Please, call me Breck."

Kade scoffed behind him. "You never let me call you by your first name."

Breck tossed a look behind his shoulder. "You were a murder suspect. Charly's a potential victim. Big difference."

"A future victim. Not potential."

His gaze swung back to her, hating the forlorn expression, the defeat in her eyes.

"I like the word potential better."

"Well, it's not accurate."

He frowned. "I didn't come here to argue with you."

"Now that's a surprise," Kade drawled under his breath.

Charly wiped her hands on a towel, then draped it across her shoulder. "Okay, so why are you here?"

"I have more questions. I'd like to start at the beginning again."

The pain that echoed in her eyes gutted him and made him hate himself that he had to put her through that torment again. But if he was to find this killer, he had to look at every angle, had to revisit the pieces over and over again until he found the anomaly.

"Do we have to?"

"I'd like to." He gestured at the utensils, bowls, and

ingredients lying before him. "Please, continue what you were doing. We can talk as you work."

She sighed but didn't move.

"This is what he does, Charly. He nags and nags and pokes and asks the same damn thing over and over."

Breck threw an annoyed look at Kade. "You can go. No need for both of us to be here."

Kade smirked. "I don't mind staying. And don't worry, Holstrom, I also told Charly you're the best at your job so she's in good hands."

Oh, but he was very worried.

Because if he couldn't find this killer before they struck again, Charly would be right. She'd be the next victim.

"It's okay, Kade. Mason called earlier and I could tell you wanted to go. Breck"—it felt funny saying his name, but she also liked the sound of it—"will be here. I'll be fine."

Kade frowned, and she wanted to wipe it off his face. They shouldn't worry about her. Not when there was nothing they could do to stop the outcome.

"Text me when you're about to leave. I don't want her alone for one second."

Breck nodded, and she rolled her eyes. She had another week before she officially died. Or did they forget that?

Kade left and silence filled the room. She continued making a mess everywhere. Too much nervous energy, especially with Donnie and Joe hovering all night and then Kade this morning. She'd decided to make cookies. Not that she was a great baker or anything. But when she had a vision on her mind, making her fret, she baked. She'd done the same thing when she had the vision of Kade getting poisoned. Hence why she delivered so many baked goods to his house when he first moved in. She wanted to keep an eye on him, plus try to figure out who had been trying to kill him.

"What are you making?"

Breck's deep voice startled her as she had been lost in thought. She smiled when she connected her gaze with his, witnessing his own gentle smile.

"Chocolate chip cookies." Then she giggled as her gaze followed his as he swept a glance across the counter. "I'm not the tidiest baker."

"Well, please, continue doing what you're doing. We can chat while you bake."

Their gazes connected again, and this time she saw what she missed when he first walked into the kitchen. The sadness.

"Did something happen today?"

He squinted as if trying to read her in return. "Your psychic abilities telling you that?"

She rested her elbows on the counter, leaning toward him, deciding this required her full attention. "No, the sad look in your eyes is telling me that. When you perfect how to avoid touching things and people, you always develop how to read them very well."

"Kade's not wrong when he says that I will nag and nag until I nag some more."

She didn't doubt that. What was the point he wanted to make?

"When you keep going over the details, new things will emerge. It helps, even if it feels like I'm being annoying."

"I came to you. I knew what I was getting into." Sort of. She'd hoped he'd take what she told him and do something with it. Not continuously bother her for details. Reliving it wouldn't help her as much as it would help him. Last night she barely slept—again.

By the tiredness evident in his eyes, he hadn't gotten much sleep either.

"When you have a vision, do you get a sense of the days in between before whatever you see happens?"

Her brows drew inward as she tried to decipher his question. "Meaning what? I don't understand."

"A man attacks you and kills you. We know this because you saw it. But do you have a sense of anything leading up to this vision? Do your visions give you details if this man followed you, was spying on you? I need to know his patterns."

Oh, how she wished she could sense those things.

"No, I don't get a sense of that. I only know what I saw, what I told you already."

"Okay, have you had a feeling anyone has been watching you? Following you?"

She understood where he was going with this line of questioning. The killer was planning before enacting her brutal death.

"No. I rarely leave the house. I haven't had any weird feelings while being at home."

"Nothing out of the ordinary? A new postal worker delivering your mail? A new person delivering your groceries? Someone new in the neighborhood? Absolutely nothing?"

The desperation in his tone made her reach out her hand. Right before she would've made contact with his hand resting on the counter, she stopped. He had his hands balled into tight fists as if he were exerting all his energy to remain calm in front of her. His gaze glided down to her gesture as if she had touched him.

"What happened, Breck? There's something you're not telling me."

His eyes flashed with terror for a brief second before veiling into the arrogant confidence she was used to seeing.

"I'm trying to find this killer. Most murders don't happen randomly."

She moved her hand back to her side of the counter, though her elbows still rested on it. Her entire body was taut with tension, but someone had to appear calm with the anxiety swirling between them. She'd pretend, if nothing else.

"I've been honest with you in every encounter we've had. I'd appreciate the same courtesy."

He narrowed his eyes as if wanting to hammer back with attitude, then he sighed, unfurling his fists.

"A new case landed on my desk today. A woman was raped and then murdered late last night. Strangled with a tie."

Charly stood up so fast, she stumbled, catching the counter behind her. Small miracle because she would've fallen if not for that. Breck raced out of his seat around the counter and nearly grabbed her by the shoulders. Her hand reaching out stopped him from that mistake.

"Charly..."

Her name whispered on his lips was something she shouldn't like. But the way he said it... It was the first time he hadn't used Ms. Yarrow to address her.

"You can't touch me, remember?"

He looked pained at the prospect, which was odd because they barely knew each other. "Well, when you almost fell, what do you expect me to do, stand there and watch you hurt yourself? Not going to happen."

She straightened, letting go of the counter for support.

Unfortunately, for her, Breck didn't get the message to move back and give her space. One more tiny step and her body would brush with his chest. It was like begging for danger.

"Can you move back, please? I'm okay. I guess I should've expected I wouldn't be the only victim."

"I believed you yesterday, yet..." He shook his head, glancing away, though he still hadn't moved back. "I didn't truly believe until this morning." His expression turned fierce. "I will not let that happen to you."

"You can't stop—" Her words broke off when his hand rose and stopped inches from her cheek. "If you touch me, I might see more things you don't want me to see."

"Don't say I can't stop this. I don't want to hear that ever again. Do you understand me?"

His demand, instead of annoying her, made her stomach flip as if tiny little butterflies were attacking her system. She didn't appreciate anyone telling her what to do. But it was the added anguish she could hear in his tone that had her belly tingling with a sensation she'd never felt before.

"Charly. I said—"

"I heard you." One demand was enough for her. Though she wasn't surprised he had continued until she agreed.

His hand still hovered near her cheek. She eyed it, wishing he'd make contact. What would it feel like to be caressed? For a man to touch her as if they couldn't help themselves? She wanted to know. To experience. To mean something to someone for once. Not for what she could do for them, but because they wanted to touch her.

Then, to her disappointment, his hand went to his side.

"What did you see yesterday when I touched you?"

She met his gaze once again. Nothing, not even the sad ache was displayed. It's as if he had forced every emotion to hide.

"Are you sure want to know?"

"We've established we only want honesty between us. So yes, I want to know."

She nodded. "She was driving and her car lost traction. It was very icy roads that night. She couldn't stop, and her car went over the embankment and into the lake, breaking the ice. She couldn't get out and she drowned. It wasn't your fault."

He swallowed hard, his eyes closing briefly before meeting hers again. "How can you say it wasn't my fault?"

"You weren't even there."

"So how can you see all of that? You're right. I wasn't there. So you shouldn't be able to see all that."

"I saw everything leading up to the accident. Then I saw you at the scene of the accident. It tells me all I need to know. It wasn't your fault."

"But I was the reason she left that night. We had said things that I know I regret. If I hadn't upset her the way I had, she wouldn't have left and died that night."

"And does blaming yourself make it easier losing the woman you loved?"

He looked confused by the question.

"Because it happened and, no matter how much you want to blame yourself, it wasn't your fault. It was an accident."

"I didn't love her." He winced. "I mean, I didn't love her the way she wanted me to. That was part of what we fought about that night. She wanted to get married, and I wanted to take a step back. Maybe if I told her—"

Charly put her hand up this time, hovering near his cheek, making him pause his words. "We both know you are a brutally honest man and she would've detected the lie as soon as you said the words she wanted to hear. She would've still left that night. It happened the way it happened because it was meant to happen. You have to stop blaming yourself for something you had no control over. The same way I need you to not blame yourself when I die."

His eyes narrowed. "I thought I told you not to speak like that."

"I forgot." Her lips twisted into a silly smile. She had forgotten that part because whatever was going on between them right now was hard to ignore. Nothing else mattered but the energy zinging to life between them. She had never wanted to touch another person as badly as she wanted to touch him. Even a little brush against his cheek.

Then he took the option away from her. He stepped back and rounded the counter, taking a seat once again.

"Now that we understand each other a little better, let's go through it again. Detail by detail. Then I need to go find this killer before he hurts another woman. Before he hurts you. I promise on my life I will not let anyone hurt you."

By the venom in his tone, she almost believed him.

5

SWEET, sultry music filled the kitchen, and she wondered if she wasn't being silly. She should change it to something pop or country. Not this sappy, do-you-want-to-kiss-me kind of music.

"What is that smell?" Bailey asked with a chipper tone as she walked into the kitchen.

The simple question distracted Charly from her internal war. She was being ridiculous. Just because Breck had come over the last two nights, didn't mean he would come tonight as well. Putting on music wouldn't tempt the man to touch her anyway. She'd scared him off the first time he touched her by seeing how his girlfriend had died tragically. What she hadn't seen was if it was recent or way back in his past.

"Pork chops with air-fried potato chips. I'm going to steam the broccoli. It should all be done soon."

Bailey sat at her island counter, while Kade chatted with Mason on the phone in the living room. They'd all had a nice routine the last few days. Kade hung out with her during the day. Around suppertime, Bailey would join them for a meal. Shortly after, Breck would show up and they would leave. He'd make her go over the details of her death, something she dreaded every night. Then they chatted about inconsequential things before he left and Donnie and Joe took over watching her house. Breck had yet to meet them, but she knew he knew they were out there. He didn't like talking about the paranormal, and she avoided it so she didn't make him uncomfortable. Why mention there were vampires outside when he already knew it?

What did it matter?

She'd be dead in a week from today. Gone from the world. Falling for an obstinate detective would *not* help her come to terms with her death.

"Has Holstrom made any progress on that woman's case yet?"

Charly had, begrudgingly, told Bailey and Kade about the murdered woman. Every evening Bailey asked the same question, as if she'd hold it in for suspense or something. If she knew something, she would've told them right away.

"No, but you know Breck, he's working hard on it."

Bailey smirked. "I don't know *Breck*. I know Holstrom though."

Charly scoffed, rolling her eyes. "Stop it. You know what I meant."

"He's never even told me to call him Breck. He likes you."

Oh, how she wished that were true. He tolerated her. They'd come to an understanding. No matter how difficult it would be, they'd always be honest with each other. She had been much better at not insisting she'd die no matter what he tried to do to change the outcome. Just because she didn't voice it didn't mean she didn't believe it. It would happen no matter what. But for his sake, since he asked, she didn't repeat it.

"As he told Kade, I'm a victim, not a suspect. Let's talk about something else."

As much as she enjoyed his visits, she didn't like the subject matter he insisted on conversing about every time. Since she still had to chat about it with him, she didn't want to do it with Bailey.

Charly turned back to the stove, ignoring the laughter in Bailey's eyes. Bailey thought Breck liked her more than a detective on a case. Not true. Charly would've sensed any attraction on his part in the last few days. She was good about reading people. When a person had to be overly aware of their surroundings, it made them hyper-aware of a lot more.

Conversation turned to Bailey and her pregnancy, which Charly was grateful for. Kade joined them soon after, and the meal was consumed. Charly liked to take care of most of the cleanup. Less chance for her to get a residual reading from one of them. She shooed them out of the kitchen.

She noticed the energy shift the moment he walked into the space. Turning around from the sink wasn't even necessary.

"Smells good in here. I'm sorry I missed it."

She was sorry she never thought to invite him. Not even one of the days. She twisted with her hands still in the sudsy water, nodding toward the fridge. "We didn't eat it all. Heat some up."

"I didn't mean you had to feed me." For the first time since she'd met him, his cheeks dusted a rosy red.

"Don't be like that, Breck. Get some food."

Argument—or whatever that was—over. He moved to the cupboard where she kept her plates, then grabbed the leftover containers from the fridge. It's as if he fit into her space without even asking where anything was. What an observant man to know where to grab everything in the few short days he'd been in her house.

Bailey and Kade walked in to say goodbye. Charly did not miss the way Bailey looked at her with the teasing sparkle, as if saying, "Look at how comfortable he looks moving around your kitchen."

"Good night, Bailey."

She giggled on her way out, and Charly couldn't help but laugh a bit herself.

"Did I miss the joke?" Breck asked as he took a seat at the counter.

"It was nothing. How's the food?"

"I'm sure it tastes delicious because it smells damn good." Then he took his first bite, and she didn't need to be a psychic to know he enjoyed it. The bliss in his eyes, the way his lips curled up in delight. He enjoyed her cooking.

"This is almost a tease. I never get good meals like this."

"You don't cook?"

He shrugged. "Sometimes, but not often. I work too much. By the time I get home, I don't have the energy to cook."

She would agree with his assessment. He worked way too much. She had no doubt he went home and still worked on his cases when he should be relaxing. It didn't take a psychic to figure that out either.

He ate in silence, moaning on occasion, telling her every time he enjoyed her cooking. She washed the dishes, not needing to fill the space with words. They were both comfortable, and she liked that they didn't need to speak.

"Why don't you have a dishwasher?"

"I do. It's right there." She tossed her head to the left where the dishwasher sat.

Breck pursed his lips in a comical way. "Then why aren't you using it?"

For one, she wanted to keep busy while he was in her kitchen. Less chance to throw herself at him. Two, she found the mundane task a nice change of pace sometimes. She didn't always wash the dishes by hand, but when she did, she enjoyed it immensely.

"Sometimes, I enjoy getting my hands wet. That's all."

She turned her head at the way he coughed. He wouldn't look her in the eye.

"You okay?"

"Yep," he responded a bit too fast. "Here's my plate. Thank you for the meal. I enjoyed every bite." He pushed his plate across the counter toward her instead of getting up and walking around to hand it to her.

She understood the need to keep their distance. The plate joined the other dishes and soon after, she had everything cleaned. Now to the dreaded part of the night.

"Do you want something to drink?"

He stared at her while she stood by the cupboard that held the wineglasses and finally nodded. "Just one."

Normally, he declined. She always had a drink when they got to this part. It helped get her through all the dreaded questions.

She poured them both a large glass, and then they took a seat in the living room. He sat on one end of the couch, and she took the other side. It was a loveseat, though, and not very large. He sat closer than she liked.

"Well, shall we start at the beginning?" Even she cringed, matching his expression, at the way she said it so chipper and giggled merrily as if she couldn't wait.

FOR THE FIRST TIME, Breck didn't want to revisit her vision. He wanted to chat with her and get to know her better.

Which was utterly ridiculous!

Not that he believed he wouldn't stop her vision. But because she was a psychic. They would never mix. Hard-nosed detective and all-seeing psychic? Yeah, that didn't sound compatible at all.

"Breck?" Charly's knuckles looked white as if she were exerting too much pressure on her wineglass. He had yet to touch his wine. Her bubbliness had disappeared in the blink of an eye.

He set his wineglass on the stand by his end of the couch. Her side had a weird-looking tree with no leaves on it. Just sporadic branches spouting out of it. He knew it was fake, but he didn't understand the point of having it. Of course, he didn't have many knickknacks scattered around his house to begin with.

He needed to keep it professional, and that's what he was going to do.

"I'm not making good headway on Carla's case. There are no witnesses for the night of the murder. She wasn't having issues with anyone, not even her boyfriend. I hate not having even an inkling. Even with Kade's wife's murder, I had a few suspects. Something to go on. This..." He thought about picking up the wineglass and downing it in one swallow.

"You put too much pressure on yourself."

He wouldn't deny that. It would be silly to pretend otherwise.

"Do you want to run through my vision now?"

He saw the heartache in her eyes. It was the last thing she wanted to do. So why make her? He didn't want to do it again either. They had been over everything the last five days since she told him and nothing new had stuck out.

"Not really."

Her eyes flashed surprise. "Oh." She sat back on the cushion, sipping her drink. "Well, then you didn't have to come over for the little update you had. You could've called me."

He had gotten her number two days ago, something he should've done right away. The temptation to reach out to her often had overwhelmed him more than he cared to admit. It was like dangling candy in front of a child knowing they wouldn't be getting a piece, no matter how much they begged.

She was right. He could've called.

Or...

He could drop the pretenses and maintain the honesty they had established in the beginning. If what she said was true—that her vision would come true no matter what—then he shouldn't waste a moment of their time together. Not that he'd ever allow her to be murdered. Over his dead body!

"What would you say if I said I like spending time with you?"

Her eyes rounded into large saucers, and he realized he should've stood up and walked away. Honesty wasn't always the best policy.

"That you're coming down with a fever."

Except she couldn't touch his forehead to double-check.

A short, defeated laugh slipped out. He pressed his hands to his knees and stood up. "It's been a long day. I should go. I'm sorry for taking over your evening once again."

She had no coffee table in front of her couch as most

people had, so he stepped forward, his strides long and determined toward the front door.

He heard a soft clink then padded footsteps trail him. Her tiny frame zoomed past his and her body blocked the door before he could grab the handle. She spread her arms wide across the door as if that would prevent him from leaving. For the most part, it would. Because he'd have to touch her to move her from the door, and nothing good came from touching her.

"Don't go. Not like this."

She wore a loose T-shirt, as usual, but he could tell she had no bra on. Also, as usual. He noticed every detail wherever he went. Call it the detective in him. But with Charly, he looked longer, more than he should. Definitely wasn't professional the way his gaze always lingered on her. The way she spread her arms open, it stretched the T-shirt across her breasts, begging his eyes to drool over the sight. He wished she'd put her arms down.

He had no idea how it happened—when it happened! But he wanted to kiss this woman more than he wanted to do anything else in his life.

It was wrong!

More than just because she was psychic.

She was also a victim in the murder case he was working on. Well, okay, not an official victim—yet.

"Breck?" she whispered desperately when he hadn't said a word.

Talk about the worst possible time to be thinking through things before speaking. She thought he was ignoring her.

He licked his lips, and she caught the movement. They were dry. He needed to apply Chapstick. But he did it again because he liked the way her eyes followed the movement as if she wanted to lick them herself.

"I should go, Charly."

"And I said not like this."

He groaned, averting his gaze. "Please put your arms down." He felt her shift and looked back at her, grateful she had listened.

She had her arms crossed now. "What would you say if I returned the sentiment?"

That she liked their time together as well?

"I don't like reliving my vision." She let her arms fall to her sides. "But I do look forward to you coming every night."

"I work too much to focus on dating. Hell, the few women I dated in the past couldn't handle my job or the odd hours." He groaned again, swiping a hand down his face. "I don't know why I'm even saying any of that. It's not like anything can happen between us."

"I know. I'm dying next Friday."

Damn her! He had told her not to say that again.

He stalked forward, eliciting a sharp cry of surprise from her lips, and boxed her in, putting his hands on the door on both sides of her. He made sure not to touch her in any way, but she had no way of escaping unless she pushed him or rubbed against him in some way.

His mouth drew closer to hers, gritting his teeth as he growled low, "Not because of that. I told you I would not let anything happen to you."

"Please move back, Breck."

"No."

She shivered, her eyes betraying her words. They sparkled with anticipation, with the desire he felt coursing through his veins as well.

"I need you to move back."

"Why?"

She blinked as if shocked by the question. "Because if you touch me or I accidentally touch you, you know I will see things you don't want me to see."

"Exactly."

"What?"

Why was she having such a hard time understanding the bottom line between them?

"Charly," he enunciated her name very slowly, "nothing can happen between us because I can't touch you without you digging into my past."

"It's not as if I want to dig into your past," she hissed.

That he believed.

"Have you ever tried to stop it from happening?"

The way she rolled her eyes said he'd asked a very stupid question. Of course she had tried.

"What about your parents? The times they hugged you or comforted you when you were ill or something?"

"Breck, you don't understand. I don't let anyone touch me. My parents knew not to do it either."

"Are you telling me no one has ever shown you any kind of affection? Not even a simple hug or a quick peck on the cheek?"

"No one. Sure, as a baby they held me, but as I grew older and started to blurt out things I shouldn't know about them, they stopped touching me. That's not to say they were horrible parents. They were so very loving. But they had to protect themselves. Nobody wants their secrets taken from them without their consent."

What a sad childhood. Not that he dared to express that.

When he didn't say anything, her gaze drew to the floor, or more like his chest because he stood so close to her.

He should move back, and yet he couldn't find the strength to do so.

"What would you do if I said I wanted to kiss you?"

Her gaze snapped up. "You can't."

"Oh, I can. I know the risks. But what would you do if I did?"

"I wouldn't return the kiss."

Well, that told him enough. She might enjoy him coming over but not enough to kiss him.

He moved away, hating how she sighed in relief when she had room to move.

"I'm sorry. That was very unprofessional of me. I won't cross the line like that again. I'm here to help you, and I will not get distracted by that again."

"Breck...I appreciate your help."

"I should go."

Something that should've happened before he revealed way too much to her.

This time she stepped away from the door and let him open it. "Umm, your night friends?"

That garnered a gentle smirk from her. "Donnie and Joe? The vampires, yes?"

Right. He would not say the word vampire under any circumstance. "I usually stay longer than this. How do I know they're here yet?"

On cue, her phone buzzed in her pants pocket. She pulled the phone out and showed him the text from Donnie.

"Okay, then. I'll see you later." He wasn't even going to ask how they knew at that exact moment to text her the answer to his question.

The see you later, he had no idea what that meant or why he said it. Tomorrow was Saturday, and he generally didn't work the weekends unless he had a tough case in front of him.

Well, Charly's impending murder was a good excuse to go into the office. It would also keep him away from her.

She didn't say anything as he walked away, and he chose to remain silent as well.

Sometimes, being honest ruined everything. He wished he would've kept his mouth shut.

6

"You look like shit, man. What's up?"

Breck looked up from his desk to Jerry, who stood eating a doughnut and getting crumbs on the papers scattered around.

"Do you mind?" Breck flicked the flecks of donut off his desk.

He wasn't about to tell Jerry why he looked like shit. Because he didn't get a wink of sleep all weekend dreaming about a woman who would never let him touch her. Or better yet, a woman he shouldn't touch if he didn't want his entire life displayed in her head without his consent.

"Sorry I asked." Jerry rolled his eyes and walked away.

Honestly, why would Breck answer his asinine question? He hadn't exactly been polite by saying he looked like shit.

Over the weekend, he'd avoided Charly like the plague. He was even proud of himself for not texting her once. Not even a simple, how are you? I miss you would've portrayed him as a lovesick puppy, which he was not!

Danielle, his ex-girlfriend, who Charly knew had died in a car crash, wouldn't even have gotten that emotion out of him. He thought more about Charly throughout the weekend, wondering how she was holding up more than he ever had about Danielle. That right there was why he'd broken things off. She hadn't been the one so why pretend otherwise.

Well, that wasn't to say Charly was the one either. She most likely was on his mind too much because of her death that loomed in a few days. Four more to be exact.

He perked up in his seat when a ping alerted him to a new email. He scanned the contents, surprised to get anything useful back concerning Kade's house.

They found a match on the blood sample belonging to Nathan Torrenson, age twenty-four. Practically a child compared to him, but old enough to know better. For someone so young, the guy had a record a mile long. Ranging from burglary to assault to misdemeanor theft. So breaking and entering an abandoned house wasn't too far off the mark for the guy.

Carla's case had grown cold. Time to move on to one that had heated up.

He grabbed his wool jacket from behind his chair and flinched in surprise when he saw Detective Stewart by his desk. He hadn't even heard him walk up to it.

"How can I help you, detective?"

"Can we drop the formalities and use our given names, considering we both use the title? I didn't realize we were back to such formalities since we've worked together before."

He wouldn't say they *worked together* on Kade's wife's murder. They chatted about it and exchanged some information, but they hadn't been partners in the matter.

Breck shrugged. "Fine by me. How can I help you, Mason?"

Mason gave him a grim expression at the way he enunciated his name but otherwise said nothing else on the matter.

"I wanted to talk to you about Kade's house. He told me what happened and I—" Mason stopped, glancing around the area, noting how many people occupied it. "Looks like you were leaving. Can we talk outside?"

Yes! The last thing he wanted to do was talk about spells and witches and shit in front of people who had no idea those things existed.

Mason followed him to his car before he started speaking again.

"Mona is working harder to find a way to close the portal."

"Good."

Nothing else had to be said on the matter. He opened his door, making Mason move back a step.

"Any news on the break-in?"

"I got the results back from a drop of blood we found at the foot of the stairs. I was going to pick the guy up for questioning."

Mason looked at the passenger-side door. "Mind if I tag along?"

He hesitated. He worked better alone. "I suppose not." But he could be a team player when need be.

They drove in silence to Nathan's house. Breck wanted to slam a hand into the wall when his mother informed him that Nathan hadn't been home all week. He could probably find him with his friend Adam Burtalli. Mason remained quiet while he looked up the friend's information. Same rap sheet as Nathan. No wonder they were friends.

He made his way to Adam's house.

"Any news on Charly's matter?"

He clenched his jaw. Not something he wanted to think about. Or her. In any sense.

"No."

"If you need help, I'd be more than happy to assist."

"No, thanks."

He vowed to keep her safe, and no way in hell he'd pass the baton on to someone else to do so.

Mason returned to being quiet.

When he knocked on Adam's door, the man himself answered. He would've darted away if Breck hadn't grabbed the front of his shirt and pulled him onto the porch and shoved him against the wall.

"Not so fast. What's the rush?"

"You can't touch me!"

Again, he wanted to punch his hand through the wall. If he wanted to touch something, he was going to damn well touch it!

"You were going to run from the police. That's suspicious. I can detain you if I'd like. Slap some resisting arrest charges along with breaking and entering."

"You didn't announce yourself as police," the annoying rat shot back. Though his eyes rang with fear when he said breaking and entering. So he'd been with his friend Nathan during the time of the break-in.

"Well, your guilty self didn't give me time. I'm Detective Holstrom, and this is Detective Stewart. We're investigating a burglary. Now why don't you tell us everything you know."

The way Adam swallowed hard, his eyes enlarging into huge saucers, Breck had no doubt in his mind Adam had the answers he sought.

"I don't know what you're talking about."

"You do," Breck stated in a tone that said he wouldn't be arguing the fact. "I haven't managed to put you at the scene of the crime, but your friend Nathan was. Undeniable proof. As of right now, I'm not even looking in your direction. I do want to talk to your friend, however."

"I don't know where he is."

Breck's lips thinned into a tight line. He didn't lose his cool often. It took a lot—and he meant *a lot*—for him to lose his shit. But with the lack of sleep all weekend, the worry building in his gut over Charly, the sexual frustration he hadn't experienced in a long time, he was riding a fine line between right and wrong. And right now, he wanted to smash his fist in this kid's face until he told him what he wanted to know.

Maybe Adam sensed the rage simmering and the way he was close to exploding.

"I swear to God I don't know where he is!" Adam cried. "I haven't seen him since last Monday. He stopped by to grab some clothes and then left. I swear I haven't seen him since."

"Is that normal behavior?" Mason asked, making Breck flinch and forgetting he had been standing next to him.

Adam shook his head. "Not really. We usually hang out every day. Hell, he sleeps at my house more than his own."

"So why do you think he disappeared?" Mason asked.

Adam shrugged. "Why should I know?"

Breck tightened his hold on the kid's shirt. "You're best friends. That's why. Did he find something in the house he broke into that made him run?"

"Ha! That place had shit in it," Adam scoffed. Then the blood drained from his face at his confession.

Yeah, these men were little boys not knowing how to grow up into law-abiding adults. Stupid to boot too.

"So you know what house I'm talking about when I say one was broken into?"

"I—"

Breck put pressure on his hand, making Adam sink deeper into the house as if he really could. "Think carefully before you lie to me."

Adam nodded. "I didn't take anything from it. I swear! The place creeped me out."

"Why?" Mason asked. Breck thought that was the world's dumbest question. He knew why it creeped him out. Hello! They conducted a weird seance of some sort in it. Of course, it was a creepy-ass house. Not to mention, Kade's wife was murdered there.

"I don't know. It was...creepy." Adam shivered as if reliving the entire thing. "It was like...there was a presence or something there. We even felt a rush of cold air at the top of the stairs."

Breck shared a look with Mason. That's where they conducted the spell.

"Did Nathan feel it too?"

"He wouldn't admit to it, but yeah, I'm sure he did."

"Then the next day, he dropped by, grabbed some clothes and you haven't seen him since?" Mason asked as if wanting to understand everything clearly. "You didn't leave that night together?"

"I told you. That place was creepy! I told him I'd wait for him outside, but it was taking him too long. I bailed before Nathan came out. I didn't see him until the next day. If he found something and took it, I wasn't there to see it."

"When did you trash the place?" Breck asked.

Adam's eyes rounded in surprise. "Dude, I didn't touch anything! Not a damn thing. If something got broken, it wasn't me."

Breck wouldn't consider *everything* to be just something. Destruction had been evident from top to bottom as if something had come over someone in a fit of rage.

"If Nathan didn't find anything, would that make him break everything? Smash the dishes? Cut up the couches? Tear the paintings off the walls?"

"Seriously? All that happened?" Adam shook his head. "Nathan can get mad and shit, but not like that."

"So you're telling me you two didn't do that?" Breck wanted to confirm.

"No," Adam pronounced it vehemently, "I'm telling you *I* didn't do that. I left before Nathan. I can't say what he might have done when I left. He was acting strange when he stopped by. It wasn't the dude I know."

Well, that was odd.

Breck didn't like any of this, especially since the house could be haunted by a vengeful spirit or something. On the day of the spell, Bailey had almost been pushed down the stairs by something. Mona had figured something might've come through the portal she opened. None of what Adam told him boded well.

"If Nathan comes by, I want to know immediately." He finally let go of Adam's shirt and took a step back, pulling out his wallet. Then he handed Adam his card.

The kid took it with a trembling hand. "So I'm not under arrest?"

Sure, Breck could arrest him based on his confession, but Kade had said he didn't care either way if they caught the people. He was starting to feel it would be better to sweep everything under the rug because of what had happened in the house months ago. First, he had to find Nathan and hear his side of things.

"Right now, you're cooperating with me. I want to find Nathan, and soon. You'll help me with that."

Adam nodded vigorously as if he were willing to throw his best friend under the bus without hesitation.

He and Mason were silent until both car doors were shut.

"Close that damn portal today!"

Mason sighed. "It seems like it might be too late."

Yeah, Breck was afraid of that. Which was why finding Nathan was imperative.

———

SHE TUCKED her legs underneath the blanket some more, then shifted again when the position still didn't feel right. The book she held wasn't holding her attention, so she slammed it to the seat cushion and leaned against the back of the couch.

He was still ignoring her. She'd acted like an idiot last Friday, and now Breck didn't even want to be in her presence.

Of course, he could be hard at work, finding the killer to her soon-to-be murder. Well, duh! He was definitely working the case, but why didn't he show up tonight? Kade spent the day with her as usual. She had needed to work out the tension that built during the weekend of not seeing or hearing from Breck. So she'd immersed herself in building another chair. The sanding had helped to stave off the anger simmering below the surface.

What had he expected asking her such a ridiculous question?

He couldn't kiss her!

She'd see things she shouldn't.

Now he was acting like the injured party, staying far away from her. Whatever.

Bailey came over for supper, but the conversation wasn't as lively as it normally was. Though Bailey was wise enough not to bring up Breck, knowing that's why Charly was in such a sour mood. They left when Donnie and Joe arrived.

The clock on the wall ticked monotonously as it sped around the circle. Eight o'clock and she was wired with more tension than she'd woken up with.

She threw the blanket off her, letting it fall to the floor, and paced the length of the room.

Maybe she shouldn't have said she wouldn't return the kiss. Lying wasn't part of their forte. They'd decided from the beginning honesty would be best.

So why had she lied?

Of course, she would've poured herself into any kiss he bestowed upon her. But pretending like she didn't want it saved both of them in the end. Why couldn't the obstinate man see that?

She screeched, placing a hand to her heart when Donnie appeared in the threshold of the room.

"Sorry." He looked repentant at the intrusion.

"You startled me, but it's okay. Everything all right?"

"You tell me. I didn't mean to walk in without an invitation, but your heart rate sped up, and I heard multiple footsteps that had me concerned."

Her pacing had alerted him? Was her heart beating erratically? She paused. Okay, yes. It was beating harder than it should. Breck's fault! He put her in this state of manic behavior.

"I'm sorry that I worried you. I have a lot on my mind."

Donnie leaned against the frame, crossing his arms. She couldn't deny he was handsome. Though she didn't know how old he was, she knew he'd been around a very long time. Since vampires didn't age, she surmised he'd died young. Early thirties. No wrinkles lined his face. No gray hair. Smooth smile. Bright green eyes—or red when his vampire senses took flight. If she wasn't already attracted to an arrogant man who thought he could prevent her death, she could find herself falling under Donnie's spell. For a vampire, he was very kind. To her, that trait went a long way more than a good-looking face ever would. Bonus points for Donnie, he had both.

"Care to share with me? I'm a good listener."

She shrugged and resumed her pacing. "Not really. It doesn't matter anyway."

"Your level of agitation says it does," he remarked as he eyed her marking her floor with too many footsteps.

His head swiveled toward the front door, his face taut with tension. Then his entire body relaxed, and a wily smile graced his lips. "I believe the source of your anxiety is about to knock."

He straightened his stance as if prepared to leave out the back.

"Stay!"

He paused, tilting his head.

"You haven't officially met Breck yet. Don't you think you should?" It didn't take a genius to know who he was talking about. Donnie was too perceptive for his own good.

She was not making an excuse to not be alone with him. What would happen anyway? Nothing! That's what. But perhaps with an audience, a vampire, no less, she wouldn't let loose all the fury that'd built during the weekend.

Why was she even mad?

Breck had every right to keep his distance. In the end, she was nothing more than a future murder victim.

A knock sounded on the door.

Donnie nodded but didn't say anything. She hadn't fooled him one bit. She smiled her appreciation as she walked past him and opened the door for Breck. He looked tired. Like he hadn't slept in days. She'd know as she'd had the same problem and the same weary look.

"Hi," he started tentatively. "Can I come in?"

"Of course." She left the door open and walked away, taking position by the couch but not sitting.

Breck eyed Donnie as he stepped into the living room.

"Breck, meet Donnie." She waved a hand in his direction where he'd taken to leaning against the frame once again.

"Hi." Again, his greeting wasn't as confident as he normally was.

Donnie grinned. "Nice to finally meet you, detective."

Breck looked from him to her, then back to Donnie. "You're usually outside. Was there a problem in here?"

Donnie shook his head. "Just chatting with Charly. She's easy to talk to. I enjoy hanging out with her."

Ugh! If she didn't know any better, Donnie wanted to try and make Breck jealous. Why?! It wouldn't work anyway. Though the way Breck narrowed his eyes and his body went rigid, maybe she was wrong in her assessment. Not that Breck would be stupid enough to attack a vampire. He would not win that fight. Not many would.

"How can I help you, Breck?"

It didn't matter how he reacted to anything. He needed to leave. She'd rather pace and stew on her anger than have him anywhere near her. The temptation was too great. She preferred not to make a fool of herself.

"I thought—"

She cried out in pain, clutching her head when a vision invaded her mind. They always came out of nowhere. They hurt as if her mind was being overtaken by an unknown entity, forcing their way in. When they hit, if she wasn't sitting down, she fell. Which she did in this instance. Except Donnie caught her before she would've hit the floor hard.

Having a vampire who was faster than the speed of light helped.

Donnie held her carefully in her arms as the vision attacked her, flashes of images and scenes speeding through her head.

Minutes ticked by. Some visions lasted a long time, others were over in less than a minute.

Then it stopped. The pain lingered. It always lingered. Like a massive headache that refused to leave.

She gradually opened her eyes to see Donnie's concerned expression. "You shouldn't have done that."

"And let you fall? Not when I'm around."

He helped her to the couch, finally letting go of her.

"You look very good for your age," she said with a tiny smile. Hoping to reduce the tension she felt and to make light of what she'd seen when he touched her.

"So you know how old am I now?" he asked with a gentle grin and a short chuckle.

"I can guess based on what you were wearing when you died." She frowned, rubbing her hand against her forehead. "I'm so sorry he didn't give you a choice whether you wanted to be turned or not. It wasn't fair."

Donnie's smile died in an instant. "No, it wasn't."

"I'm sorry."

"Please do not apologize, Charly. For my past or for what happened to me. I also don't want you to apologize that I touched you. I would pick saving you from hurt over anything else. Of course, my past isn't the issue I'm concerned about. You had a vision."

Breck cleared his throat as if reminding them he was also in the room. Charly looked at him, noting he hadn't moved from his spot.

"Yes, I did."

"And?" Breck demanded. Then he smoothed out his irate features, trying again. "Tell us about it."

Though that also came out more demanding than anything.

Oh, no. Nope! She would not be sharing this vision with anyone. At least, not with Donnie in the room.

Because what she had seen scared her more than the vision of her death.

7

HE WANTED to rush to her side and pull her into his arms. Take away the torment that echoed in her eyes. Of course, he couldn't do that. Not unless he wanted her to see more of his past. And not if he didn't want to risk his life. The hard glare in the vampire's eyes unnerved him.

Damn that man! Beast! Whatever he wanted to call him. When he saw Charly start to collapse, he wanted to run to her rescue. He didn't get one step in her direction before a blur went by him and Charly was in Donnie's arm. Talk about fast as lightning.

"It's all right, Charly. Take your time," Donnie coaxed, sending another stern gaze his way.

What did he do? He hadn't done anything wrong. Though he didn't want to be in a vampire's sights. Not for anything.

"It wasn't a big deal. It was nothing," she murmured, rubbing her forehead again.

"It knocked you on your ass."

She looked up at him, frowning. Okay, he could be a little gentler in his tone. What did she expect? He was going out of his mind with worry. He'd never seen anyone have a vision before. She looked like she had been in excruciating pain, as if someone had been torturing her. Then, to top it off, the damn vampire came to her rescue instead of him!

"They always hit me hard. They come so unexpectedly. I'm okay, though. I really am."

Donnie nodded, then turned to leave. "I'll let you rest. Say my name if you need me, otherwise I will remain out of sight for the remainder of the evening."

"Thank you, Donnie. You're such a kind friend. I appreciate everything you're doing for me."

"That's what friends do."

Breck blinked and the man had disappeared. Freaky! He'd take Mona the witch over spending time with a vampire anytime.

Then he sought out Charly again and decided he was done being so far away from her. He stalked to the couch in three long strides and took a seat next to her. Close enough where he could pull her into his arms if he wanted to tempt fate. But enough space where they didn't actually touch.

"Tell me about your vision." His voice was much quieter and softer, hoping that would help her talk to him.

She didn't look up. "It's not important."

"It is to me."

Her head twisted in his direction. "It has nothing to do with the murder."

"It doesn't make it any less important. It hurt you." Breck lifted his hand, aching to wrap it around her neck and pull her closer. Brush his lips against hers. Take some of the pain out of her violet eyes. Odd. He'd never noticed her eyes were damn near the color purple. Being so close, he could see it so vividly.

"I'm okay now." She shifted her gaze to his hand that still hung in the air. "Put your hand down, Breck."

Yes, of course. They'd been over this situation before. The main reason he stayed away all weekend—and almost tonight. But he lost the battle to stay away any longer. He had to see her. To know she was okay with his own eyes.

His hand dropped to his knee. "Why won't you tell me about your vision? Look, I'm sorry about the other night. I crossed a line, and it won't happen again." At least, he'd try his damndest not to let it happen again.

"Water under the bridge." She smiled as if that would make it all better. Part of his heart soared with happiness at seeing the lovely affection on her face. But he couldn't forget how she'd cried out in pain and crumbled in Donnie's arms.

"So—"

"Did you work this weekend?" She cut off his further badgering on the topic.

It wouldn't deter him.

"I did. Not much was gained on the murder front. I have a suspect on Kade's burglary though." Not that he wanted to get on that topic.

"Oh, that's wonderful."

Not really.

She must've deduced that when he didn't smile or heartily agree with her it wasn't that wonderful.

"What happened?"

"Remember they conducted that weird spell there?" They, as in Mona and Mason. Yeah, he was clumping those two lunatics together.

"I do. You were there as well."

He shivered thinking about it. "Bailey nearly fell down the stairs. Something pushed her." Charly frowned but nodded, indicating she knew that. "Mona opened a portal or something. I'm afraid that something might've..."

What was he saying? This was all insane.

"You think the burglary is linked to the spell?"

"No. Not totally. I do fear my suspect picked the wrong house to break into. We can't seem to find him, and his friend said he was acting odd after the fact."

"And that something that escaped the portal has hurt him."

"Or possessed him." Breck shook his head, denying the accusation as soon as it left his mouth.

"It's possible."

"Don't confirm my suspicions."

She giggled, and despite the reason for it, he loved her laugh.

"Bad things happen. As much as you want to deny it, the paranormal world exists. Most people live in bliss, not knowing about it. But you do. That will make your job easier."

"It doesn't feel like it." He moved his hand from his knee to the cushion, barely an inch between him and her thigh.

Her eyes caught the movement. "That's not a good idea, Breck."

"I want to know about your latest vision."

Her gaze lifted to his. "That's not a good idea either."

Why, damn it!

"You're not going to tell me?"

"Well, since you're under the impression they don't necessarily come true, it doesn't matter what it was. It's best you don't know about it."

"Well, that doesn't ease my mind." What could she have possibly seen? She claimed it wasn't related to her murder. What about then?

"Sometimes, it's better to not know the future."

"Charly, when it comes to you, I want to know everything." And didn't that just say he was crossing the line again.

"You should go, Breck."

No matter how many times he crossed the invisible line, she'd keep pushing him back across it.

He couldn't win with her.

"If not me, you should at least tell one of your friends. Like Bailey." Not the vampire. Anyone but him.

She flashed a tired smile. "This one is harmless. I'll keep it to myself."

Harmless. Ha! Nothing about what she endured was harmless. He'd bet his life whatever it was would impact both their lives. Only he wasn't sure if it would be in a good way or a bad one.

HIS HAND BRUSHED up her side and through her hair before gripping it. His tongue was doing the most amazing thing to her nipple. Swirling, sucking, and even a little nibble that had her arching her back.

"Yes, Breck!"

She felt his smile against her breast then witnessed it for herself when he lifted his head.

"You like that, uh?"

"I love it," she whispered breathlessly, eliciting a low moan when his cock rubbed against her.

"Are you ready for more?" He leaned down, caressing her lips with his. "For all of me?"

"I think I've been ready my whole life for you."

His handsome features lit up with pleasure, then he

positioned himself to dive deep inside her, his grip still wrapped around her hair.

"I promise not to hurt you."

Then he—

She sat up, heaving large breaths to the point she found it difficult to draw in the appropriate amount of air.

"Charly?"

Her gaze whipped to her bedroom doorway, knowing it was Donnie, not only by the sound of his soft voice, but his eyes were glowing red.

"You startled me again."

He stepped into the room, and she still had a hard time making his features out. The glowing eyes were a bit creepy.

"You had me worried again. I heard you cry out."

Sweat had developed all over her body, and her blankets were all twisted. The dream she'd been having—about Breck, no less—had her writhing in her bed like a bitch in heat. How embarrassing. She wasn't about to admit anything to Donnie either.

"Nightmare. I'm okay."

It wasn't a total lie calling it a nightmare. Because what she'd been dreaming had been the vision she had earlier that evening.

Her and Breck as lovers. In this very bed she lay in now.

Her body tingled from the aftereffects. From a simple recall of her vision! She couldn't imagine what his actual touch would do to her.

That was the problem. That vision could not come true. He couldn't touch her and vice versa. He'd hate her in the end for everything in his past she'd see. All his secrets out in the open.

"Your heart is still pounding."

She groaned and picked up one of her pillows, throwing

it at Donnie. "Stop listening to my heart and honing in on my agitation. It's annoying."

He had the audacity to chuckle. "You should call him."

"Stop telling me what to do too."

"I'm not a psychic like you, but I know attraction when I see it. Why hold yourself back?"

She grabbed a different pillow and shoved it in front of her, wrapping her arms around it. "I can't touch him without seeing everything. He'd hate it. He'd hate me." Her head fell to the top of the pillow. "I'll be dead in three days anyway."

The clock on her nightstand said it was Tuesday, even though night still penetrated the sky.

"You are not dying on my watch. So, therefore, you are not dying at all."

Yeah, Breck held the same notion. That her vision could turn in a different direction. Well, she'd test the theory. She'd simply stay away from Breck and not allow her latest vision to come true either. It stood to reason they had sex before she died—which would be on Friday. So from now until Friday they slept together. If she maintained her distance, it wouldn't happen, which would tell her that her murder could also be thwarted.

"What is that beautiful mind of yours thinking?"

"That you should stop coming to my rescue when my heart rate picks up a little bit of speed. You would've heard someone entering the house before my heart rate went wacko. So you know I wasn't in any serious distress."

Donnie didn't respond at first.

What could he say anyway? Everything she said was true. He came inside her house because he wanted to, not because he feared she was in danger.

"You're not the first psychic I've met."

That perked her up. She lifted her head from the pillow. "And?"

"And she has visions as well. They hit her as hard as yours do. Isabella Thorn. Her brother is psychic as well. Odd fellow, but good to have on your side."

"What's the point you're trying to make?"

"She had a vision once. Deadly, like yours. Yet she's still around to tell stories about it." Donnie turned around. "Call him. You'll sleep better if you do."

Then he was gone.

It wasn't possible. Her visions always came true. Always.

Again, she'd attempt to prove their theory right that she could stop the vision from happening. She only had to keep her distance from Breck. If they didn't sleep together then she'd believe her death wouldn't happen as well.

Knowing she'd never get any more sleep in the bed where she had erotic dreams of Breck, she got up and dressed.

Her cheeks flamed with heat. If she had a mirror, she knew they'd be beet red. She slept naked. Donnie had walked into her bedroom. The covers had been off her before she'd put the pillow to her chest. Even though it'd been dark, she knew his vision was impeccable.

"You better not have taken a peek at my naughty bits, Donnie."

She waited for him to reappear and assure her he hadn't. Then she chuckled at her ridiculousness. She was still naked! Of course, she didn't want him coming back to her room right now.

"Forget I said anything."

Then she grabbed a tank top and a pair of sweats and got dressed. She flicked on the living room light but didn't turn on the TV. She'd read more of her book.

At some point, the words blurred and she fell asleep on the couch. When she awoke the next morning, she had a crick in her neck and a small ache in her back. Added to the headache that still lingered from her vision, she was cranky. A shower didn't help with any of the pain. Nor did the medication she took. Even two cups of coffee didn't help her mood.

Kade arrived before the sun appeared, relieving Donnie and Joe. The man was smart enough not to comment on the even darker circles under her eyes and her sour mood.

"Do you mind coming with me to Mona and Mason's place?" Kade asked after breaking the silence since he entered her home.

She'd made them eggs and bacon, but they'd been quiet in the kitchen the entire time.

"I only ask because Mona's working on a spell to close the portal and I'd like to help since it involves my house."

She preferred to stay in her domain. Away from people and the potential things she could see if she stepped into someone else's house. She was used to Kade and Bailey's house across the street. Once she touched something and saw whatever there might be to see, she didn't see anything again. So she knew where it was safe to touch in their place. Mona's was unknown territory.

"I'd rather not. We know my murder happens at night. I'm safe here during the day." She pushed his finished breakfast plate to his side of the counter, ignoring his heavy sigh. "I'd like the time alone. I didn't ask any of you to keep me safe, and it's clearly eating in on things you could be doing. Don't let me stop you."

"Charly—"

"Don't. Please, Kade. Don't argue with me. Go to Mona's.

Come back if you'd like. But I want the house to myself for a while."

Kade knew she wouldn't be swayed in the matter. The determination in her eyes was easy to read. The man was wise enough not to argue and left after eating.

She wasn't afraid of dying. And she had nothing to fear during the day. Her vision had been clear. She would be murdered at night.

She flipped the lock and decided to clean her house. Anything to keep her mind off the man that still swarmed her mind and made her body tingle with desire.

8

IT TOOK MORE strength than he cared to admit for him not to slam the door on his way out. He couldn't blame the manager of Carla's building that he had no new information to share. But, like Breck did with all his cases, he revisited, re-interviewed, and re-looked a billion times before that one thing stuck out and helped him solve a case. Normally, he needed that one thing to pop out when the lack of evidence didn't help.

He glanced at his watch draped on his left wrist, groaning. He was due at Mason's house soon to...fix the problem at Kade's house. He hoped Mona knew what she was doing this time and closed...whatever she had opened the proper way.

He yanked open his car door and paused before sliding in. A yoga studio, which looked fairly new, sat across the street from the apartment complex. Deciding he hadn't questioned anyone there yet, he ventured toward the building instead of getting on the road.

A young woman with dark-brown hair pulled into a tight ponytail smiled at him when he walked inside.

"Welcome to Stretches and More. How can I help you? Are you here to sign up for our many yoga classes or more on the weight training side of things?"

He appreciated she didn't assume he'd want weight training over yoga. He knew a few guys at the precinct who loved yoga. Said it made their body feel better than it had in years.

While the pain in his back had dissipated, he wondered how much yoga would help.

What the hell was he thinking? He wasn't here to sign up for anything.

He flashed his badge and widened his smile when hers vanished. "Detective Holstrom. I'm here to ask some questions about the other night."

She nodded. "That poor woman who was murdered. She took a few classes here. She liked coming Wednesdays, but sometimes she popped in on Thursdays."

Well, he was glad he followed his gut. He removed his notepad from his jacket pocket and jotted down the information.

"Did she come with anyone?"

"Usually her friend Lisa. They seemed close."

Yes, he'd spoken to Lisa. She couldn't report any problems Carla had with anyone.

"When does your place close?"

"Eight o'clock most nights. We do stay open until nine on Fridays."

"Did you notice anyone odd or out of place on Monday?" Carla had been murdered early Tuesday morning so if anyone had been hanging around, maybe she had seen them.

"No," she replied, shaking her head. "Of course, I also don't have time to stare out the window. So if anyone was hanging around outside, I wouldn't have noticed."

Breck pulled out one of his cards and handed it to her. "If you think of anything, even something you might think is nothing, call me."

He didn't add he'd stop by again and ask more questions. Same ones as before. Because that's what he did. Sometimes, it jogged someone's memory. But most times it antagonized people and made him the bad guy.

Not too long after, he arrived at Mason's house. He eyed the creepy-looking structure, wondering if he wasn't making a mistake coming here. Who decided black was the color to go for a house? Because it'd be the last color he'd pick.

The dark, foreboding house could use some upkeep to the outside, not that he was judging. He had a few things he could do to his house as well. New gutters, probably a new roof. And his landscaping was nothing to talk about, so he wasn't one to judge. But the Halloween decorations...they didn't help the thought that this place was haunted. Because the ghostly face peeking out of the window at the very top of the house gave him the shivers.

That was only the start of the creepiness.

The yard was packed with decorations galore, from skeletons to coffins to a disturbing creature he didn't even want to guess at that stood right by the front door where he had to wait by it after he pushed the doorbell.

He wondered again why he agreed to come. Mason better be ready to close the damn portal because he didn't want to stay long. The man himself answered the door.

"Anything new to report?" Mason asked, closing the door behind him.

He was glad to see the inside of the house wasn't as dolled up as the outside.

"No. I stopped by—" Breck froze when a wolf walked into the area and sat down in front of him. He'd seen the animal before at Kade's house when they had performed that weird spell. Though he'd been in its presence, he never questioned why a wolf had been there—and so friendly. It was a wolf! Not to mention, the spell at the time had taken precedence over anything else.

"Meet Bozo."

"Is that a wolf?" He had to make sure he wasn't wrong in his assessment.

Mason nodded, then rubbed Bozo's head. "He's friendly. He won't bite."

Then a black cat raced down the stairs and took a spot next to Bozo. Yep. He remembered that animal as well. Though the cat hadn't alarmed him as much as the wolf had.

Meow.

Mason nodded again, this time as if addressing the cat, and then looked at him. "Mona's in the kitchen."

"Did you just nod at your cat?"

"His name's Scatter, and yes."

"Like you understood what he said?"

"Yep."

Breck eyed him critically, wondering if he should turn around and leave. He and the Mona woman were too much for him sometimes. This whole paranormal world was.

"What did he say?"

Mason smiled. "You don't want to know."

Then Mason headed toward what he assumed was the kitchen. He followed, making a wide berth around the animals and glancing behind him a few times before paying attention to what was in front of him.

When he walked into the kitchen, it looked like something had exploded. Contents of varying degrees covered all the counters, and red-looking gunk spattered part of the walls.

But what raised his hackles was Kade standing on the other side of the room.

"Is Charly here?"

Kade met his worried gaze. "She's at home."

"Do not tell me she's alone."

The wince that touched Kade's face told him what he didn't want to hear.

"What the hell is wrong with you?"

"Hey," Kade started. "She asked me to leave. She made a good point. It doesn't happen in the daytime. She's safe right now."

"She's in danger. She should not be alone at all."

"I've known her longer than you. I was friends with her first. I know when she's okay and when she's not," Kade shot back.

He gritted his teeth, holding back the rest of his anger. Nothing nice would come out, so sometimes it was better not to say anything at all. He looked at Mona, who kept glancing between the two of them with a piece of licorice dangling from her lips. Mason stood silently by her, not appearing concerned in the least.

Was he the only one petrified for Charly's safety?

Maybe he was. They hadn't seen Carla's dead body. They hadn't seen the vacant look in her eyes. The bruises down below that said the killer had not been gentle. The red, angry marks around her neck where the tie had strangled her.

"You can all handle this"—he waved his hand around at the mess—"without me. I'm going to Charly's."

No one said anything as he stalked out of the room, and

no one followed him either. His stride jerked when he saw the animals in the same position he'd left them. Then he corrected his stance and continued on his way, ignoring the lone meow that echoed behind his back.

Sorry. He didn't speak cat.

Though he didn't throw on his lights and sirens—but heavily tempted to—he sped the entire way to her house.

He banged on the door when he heard loud music. Why was the music so loud? He'd never heard Charly turn the volume up like this. Was she alone? Was she okay?

Preparing to lift his leg and kick open the door, it swung open. Charly frowned, eyeing him up and down.

So he probably looked manic. Leg lifted, standing on one foot. Eyes wide and filled with fright. Rigidity in every facet of his body. He couldn't explain to her—hell, even himself—the high anxiety that hit his veins when Kade said she was alone.

Before she could speak, he rushed forward and grabbed her arms, gripping hard and nearly shaking her.

"What is wrong with you?"

Her mouth dropped open, then her gaze veered left and right as she looked at his hands covering her arms. She wore a sweatshirt, so he couldn't feel her skin that he no doubt knew would be soft.

"Did you hear me?"

She blinked rapidly as if realizing she'd zoned out or something. "What are you doing here?"

She should know what he was doing here.

And why wasn't she demanding he let go?

"What are you seeing right now?"

Her brows drew low as if confused by the question.

His fingers dug into her arms to help her figure it out. He saw the light dawn in her eyes. "It only happens skin to skin. I'm not sensing anything from you right now because my sweatshirt is in the way. But you should let go."

Well, that was news to him. She made it seem like he couldn't touch her at all. No part of her, even clothes.

But, because he didn't like the slight fear in her eyes as if he'd hurt her, he let go. "Let me inside."

She crossed her arms and pursed her lips. "You're very demanding. I don't appreciate it."

"Please," he muttered through clenched teeth.

She rolled her eyes but turned around and didn't slam the door in his face, so he followed her inside, closing and locking it himself.

He slipped off his shoes as she walked away to the living room. He'd be staying a while if Kade wasn't going to be around. The music drifted away, but when he walked inside the living room, he still heard it on low volume. So she decided not to turn it all the way off.

The vibes coming from her were easy to read. Get out. Leave me alone. Stop bothering me.

Too bad.

He wasn't leaving her alone until the killer was caught. Either he'd be here, Kade would, or even the damn vampires. But she would never be by herself.

"So what's your problem now?"

He knew she didn't want to hear that he relished the idea that he could touch her with a layer of clothes between them. That was a huge problem. Knowing he could touch her wasn't off-limits. But, of course, that wasn't the real problem at hand.

"Kade left you alone. You let him."

"It's daylight. Nothing's going to happen during the day."

"Charly, it's not safe."

"If that's the only reason you came over, it was a wasted trip. You should go."

"You keep telling me that, and I hate it every time."

She sighed. "I'm seriously regretting coming to you about my vision. This is not how I wanted my last days to play out."

He clenched his jaw hard, praying he'd keep his anger in check. His hands balled into tight fists. He exerted so much energy to think his words through before speaking that Charly could see so clearly the torture he was in.

She stepped closer, her eyes sparkling with regret. The same regret she'd just announced.

"I'm sorry I said that."

"You're being honest." He appreciated the honesty more than anything, even if it did anger him.

"You're supposed to be at work. Kade will be back before it's dark. I promise you I'll be fine."

He reached up and brushed her arm. She shivered at the touch. "Well, I'm not. I can't leave knowing you're alone. I'll go out of my mind with worry. I won't get a damn thing done."

His hand sought the other arm, caressing it the same way he had the first time. Another shiver hit her body.

"I can't sleep at night thinking about you. Wondering how you're doing. Hating myself for making you mad. For constantly crossing a line I told you I wouldn't."

He lifted his hand to touch her arm again and she took a step back, preventing him from doing so.

"You shouldn't do that."

"What's the harm? You can't see my past when I do." A wicked grin touched his lips. "If you keep insisting I shouldn't do this and shouldn't do that, I'm going to say you shouldn't have told me I could touch you as long as it's not skin-to-skin."

Panic fluttered in her eyes.

Regret hit his system. "But I won't touch you if it bothers you. I'd never hurt you, Charly."

Her bottom lip wobbled. "I know that, Breck. You have no idea how much I know."

He frowned. "What does that mean? And please don't cry. I didn't come here to make you cry."

Her lip stopped wobbling, but the sadness still coated her eyes. "If you want to stay, fine. I'm cleaning the house, and I'd like to get back to that."

He knew a losing battle when he saw one.

"Okay." He paused, grateful to see some of the sadness leave her features. "I'll help you."

HE'D HELP HER? Clean her house?

When he removed his wool coat, then his suit jacket, and rolled up his sleeves, she knew he wasn't messing with her. He was going to help her.

Not exactly what she wanted. Cleaning aided her mind to stay clear of Breck. Now here the obstinate man stood, and cleaning wasn't going to do the job any longer.

She assigned him the bathroom, grinning too hard when he looked appalled at the prospect. But he didn't voice his displeasure. He got down to business, scrubbing the toilet as if it were his life's mission.

She ventured upstairs to her spare room to change the sheets and mop the floors. Not that either thing had to be done, but she'd said she wanted to clean, so she'd get this house looking so damn shiny not a drop of dust could be found.

The music resumed its loud volume, and she couldn't hide the smile that he had turned it back up for her. For the next hour, her mind, surprisingly, emptied of everything. Her problems. Her worries. Anything about Breck.

It didn't all come rushing back until she turned around from putting her freshly washed clothes in her dresser away. Breck stood a foot away. His face was flushed as if he'd put more energy than was necessary into scrubbing everything. He'd removed his tie and suit jacket, and parts of his white dress shirt had water spots. His sleeves were also halfway rolled up, giving off a lovely view of his muscular forearms.

"The bathroom is finished and I did the dishes. By hand." His triumphant smile made her match his.

"Thank you. I do appreciate the help."

His smile remained, but his forehead wrinkled a bit as if he wanted to frown.

A glance at the clock on her nightstand said lunch had passed. She hadn't eaten and could only assume Breck hadn't either. She imagined Kade would be back soon as well.

"Are you hungry?"

His eyes flashed with desire. "Very."

Images of her vision from last night danced before her, making her body tingle in places she wasn't used to feeling any kind of sensation from.

Sadly, she was a novice in all kinds of pleasure between a man and a woman. When one grew up fearing the touch of another, it robbed a person of so much. She couldn't even remember what a hug felt like. It'd been so long since her parents had bestowed one on her. And anyone else, she'd never given them the chance to hug her. Not even Bailey, and she sensed the urge in her one too many times to give her one.

Breck moved closer, barely leaving an inch between them when she didn't do anything but stare at his intense one-word response.

"You're too close." And she'd taken off her sweatshirt when she'd gotten hot. Only a tank top remained.

"Well, when you look at me like you're dying for me to touch you, I can't help myself."

She licked her bottom lip. His eyes followed the movement.

"Don't do that, Charly."

"Breck..." Her vision flashed again.

"Yes?" The ache in his eyes to reach out was so strong she knew he'd cave soon.

See. She knew it was inevitable for every vision she ever had to come true. She'd told herself to keep her distance, prove one vision could be stopped, and instead, she was allowing it to get to the precipice.

"Is it possible to have sex with clothes on?"

That had him flinching as if surprised by the question. Well, so was she. She had no idea why she'd blurted that out.

"I mean, yeah. But there will still be skin on skin. Some parts of the body have to be uncovered." His lips curled into a sexy grin. "Are we having a conversation where we're shoving the line way out of the picture?"

"No." She shook her head, took a step back, and ran into her dresser. It left her no escape. But based on her clipped answer, he didn't move toward her.

"Okay, there's no sense denying there is attraction between us," she stated, waving a hand back and forth between them. "But you answered a very good question. You know you can touch me anywhere clothes cover and it's not a big deal. Fine. But no sex can be had without skin on skin and to do so, you'd have to let me see everything. I touch something or someone and I get a flash of their past. To have sex, I'd have to touch you for a very long time and I'd no doubt see everything. You don't want that. No one would want that."

Based on the frown that punctured his features, he hadn't thought that far ahead.

"Okay." He nodded. "Then let's get the secrets out of the way."

What did he mean by that?

"My parents are divorced, and it wasn't pretty. My dad drank too much, and it caused problems everywhere. He has several DUIs and a few other arrests on his record. My mom was a saint for putting up with him as long as she had. I have a brother and a sister that I rarely see. We get together on holidays, but that's about it. I'm not close with my family and I can't say why. It sort of morphed into that.

"My job isn't easy, and I've seen too much shit that it's hard not to take it home. Maybe that's why I can't keep a girlfriend and I distance myself from my family. You already know about my girlfriend who died. Not many people know unless I tell them, which I don't. I'm a private person. I don't have any friends. So, I guess you could call me a loner. My job consumes most of my life, and it has never bothered me to be alone until I met you.

"I've found it hard to sleep the last few nights thinking about you instead of my mind absorbing my cases. That's a first. That's what tells me that I can't ignore what I'm feeling for you. I'm scared to let you in, but I'm also willing to try. I have no dirty secrets in my past that I'm worried about you seeing."

He blew out a heavy breath, then snapped his fingers. "Oh, and if you're curious as I've had the annoying question asked too many times to count, I even got into a few fights in school growing up because of it. My parents originally picked out Brock for my name. My father has atrocious handwriting, not to mention, he was drunk the day he filled out the paperwork. No surprise there. The person who recorded my birth certificate thought it was an e instead of an o, and the name Breck came alive. My father refused to have it changed, insisting that's what my mother wanted instead of owning up to his idiotic mistake."

Her heart beat rapidly at his confessions, grateful Donnie wasn't around to mention her irregular beat again.

Did he really understand what he was asking of her?

He took a step forward.

No, he didn't understand.

"Your turn."

She blinked in surprise. "It doesn't work that way. You're not going to see my past when you touch me."

"Exactly. So you have to share it with me. Just as I shared with you. Sure, you might see more than I talked about. I gave you the quick version, but there's nothing I'm worried about you knowing. If you're worried about secrets between us, then let's eliminate that problem."

But if she did that, then her vision would come true! Which meant her murder would also happen. Why couldn't he see that? Well, partly because he had no idea what her vision last night entailed.

"Charly. It's your turn." He glanced away, shaking his head. "Unless this is one-sided. I want you more than you want me."

Before he could turn around and walk away—something she sensed he was about to do—she slapped a hand to his chest. He froze.

"It's not one-sided. I won't explain again why anything happening between us would be a mistake."

The way he clenched his teeth and a muscle ticked rapidly on his cheek said she had been wise not to voice the vision of her murder. He'd never think it could come true.

"I had a sheltered childhood. Not much affection at all, for good reason. My parents did the best they could despite the circumstances. I was homeschooled and never minded it. I didn't know what I was missing. My parents died in a car crash, and I was forced into foster care at the age of sixteen. Those two years were the worst years of my life. Pretending I didn't know anything about anyone was hard. I had to go to public school and didn't have any friends. I was the weirdo and freak to everyone. I managed to avoid having any visions in front of anyone. Maybe that was a higher power saving me from humiliation.

"Once I turned eighteen, I left. I moved around a lot trying to find my place in the world. It was easier to portray a bubbly personality than to show everyone the real me. The one who hates leaving her house and talking to people. The one who fears what she might see about someone.

"I have tried telling the police about certain visions and no one has ever taken me seriously. I was a suspect in one murder five years ago when my vision came true and they demanded to know how I knew everything. Once they found the actual killer, I left town and never looked back. It was the last time I ever tried telling the police anything."

"Until me," Breck whispered, standing as frozen as a statue.

"Yes. Until you. I've never been as attracted to someone as I am with you. Breck,"—she applied pressure to his chest

—"I've never even kissed a man. Which should tell you that I've never..." Oh, this was harder than she thought. To say the words...

"You've never slept with anyone either," he finished for her.

She nodded.

He lifted his hand but didn't cover hers. "Why don't we start with a hug and go from there? You say you've never touched anyone for a long period of time. So let's experiment with that. Let me hold you, Charly. Let me show you what you've been missing out on. Hell, I haven't had a hug in a long time either."

"Okay." The word fell out breathlessly.

His hand closed around hers, then his other arm pulled her closer and tucked her into his embrace. Flashes of images and scenes from every aspect of his life flooded her mind.

And she let it. She absorbed it.

She let go for the first time in her life.

9

He could feel her trembling in his arms. Deciphering why was difficult to do. Because she was seeing things that horrified her about him? Because she wanted to pull away, the touching too much for her already? Because she enjoyed it —like he did.

She fit perfectly. Every contour of her body molded into his as if they'd been made for each other. He wasn't a guy who ever thought in that sense. Nobody would ever accuse him of being a romantic or having an overactive imagination.

The longer they held each other, the more he swore he could sense her feelings seeping through. Deciphering the slight trembles still wracking her body as...acceptance.

Time passed, and it didn't bother him they hadn't moved a muscle. For once in his life, he was living in the moment. He wasn't letting any outside interference mess with him. Work had been his sole focus for so long, being still and silent for no reason was odd. But enjoyable. He needed to do this more often.

Charly pulled away first, though he didn't let her

completely escape. His one free hand still held her back, but they had space between their bodies. Their hands were locked together on his chest.

She gripped his waist, bunching his shirt into a fist. "We're touching our hands together."

"We are." He grinned. "We also hugged. My face touched your face."

"I'm..." A beautiful smile emerged, one that he'd never seen before. It brightened her features with a happiness that he guessed she didn't feel very often.

"Yes?" he coaxed her to finish whatever was on the tip of her tongue.

"I saw a lot." Her smile didn't dim even a tiny bit. "I saw everything you told me, and other things you didn't."

"I have nothing to hide from you."

"I'm not seeing anything anymore. I feel the warmth from your hand. That's it." She giggled, her smile expanding even more. A true, honest giggle. Not one of those fake, bubbly giggles she liked to portray. To hide her real self from the world.

"Well, what do you know? Funny how that worked. We got the hard part over with."

She bit her lip. "As a child, before we understood anything, I would still see things. I was like four or five and had a fever. My mom held me through most of the night. I saw a lot. That young, I didn't understand anything. And after a while, I didn't see anything. I just felt my mom holding me."

"That sounds like a good thing."

"And then two weeks later, she felt my forehead when I looked a little flush again, worried the sickness was back. I saw more flashes of things she'd experienced in those two weeks. Her talking to my dad about me. About the things I said to her. Things I shouldn't know about her. How it frightened her. That's around the time they stopped touching me. Comforting me."

The happiness he'd witnessed moments before was gone.

"Breck, tomorrow you could come back and I'll see something new. Maybe a conversation you had with someone else about me. Maybe things you don't want me to know. *This* hard part might be over. But it'll never be over."

"You're not going to scare me into stopping touching you." He wrapped his hand tighter around hers so she'd get the message. "I like how you feel in my arms. I'm not giving that up for anything. We've already established that only honesty and no secrets are allowed between us. So I'm not worried you'll see me talking about you to someone because I won't have anything bad to say about you."

She either didn't know what to say or she was contemplating the right words to get through his thick skull that this still wasn't a good idea. She could say whatever she wanted. It wouldn't sway his mind. Once he got an idea in his head, it couldn't be changed. Kade would know. He'd understand. He'd thought Kade killed his wife. He never let up until he'd been proven wrong. He'd earned every nickname ever uttered about him. Bulldog. Asshole. Annoying. Arrogant.

"Well, as long as you know it won't ever stop."

"We're on the same page, Charly." A wicked grin hit his lips. "So can we try something else now?"

"Like what?"

Instead of saying it, he decided to show her. He bent his head and brushed his lips against hers. The soft, airy moan that fell from her lips had him increasing the pressure. They finally let their hands depart from his chest. She wrapped her arms around his waist, and he pulled her closer to him as well. One hand ventured to her silky blonde strands and held her head in place as he traced his tongue across her mouth.

"Open your mouth, Charly. Let me in."

"I don't know what I'm doing, Breck," she whimpered, as if embarrassed by her lack of skills.

Tiny kisses smothered her mouth, as he whispered between each delicate peck. "That's why I'm here to tell you what to do. Open your mouth and let me in."

Her mouth fell open with a soft breath escaping as she did so. He didn't hesitate to swoop in with his tongue. He tried to teach her with each sweep of his tongue against hers how to do it in return. His Charly wasn't stupid. She was a quick learner. The kiss started tentative and light and turned hot and heavy within less than a minute.

He found himself moving them until her back hit the dresser. Without breaking the kiss, he cupped her ass and lifted her, making her wrap her legs around his waist. His cock, hard and ready, wanted to dive deep inside her. He wanted their clothes to disappear and nothing but skin-to-skin until they were both sated with bliss.

He rocked into her, letting her feel how much he wanted her. How hard she made him with nothing more than her sweet, innocent kisses. His mouth pulled away from her lips and trailed across her chin. She leaned her head back to allow him access to her neck and her shoulder, leaving a blazing trail of kisses across her skin.

"Oh, Breck! I had no idea I could feel like this."

"I haven't even shown you half of how you could feel, sweetheart," he whispered into her ear, before nipping it then soothing it with a kiss.

He grinded against her again, eliciting an erotic moan

that lit his body even more on fire. He twisted around, and within two long strides, his legs hit the bed. Lowering her until her back hit the sheets, he paused, digging his hand into her hair once more. He fisted it as if part of him sensed he had to hold her in place in case she let the fear win and tried to dash away.

"Breck?" Her heavy breaths filled the quiet room.

They hadn't been exerting that much energy, but he understood why she felt out of breath. He could feel his lungs needing more air.

"Yes, sweetheart?"

"I—"

Whatever she was about to say was interrupted by a loud pounding on the door downstairs.

She giggled, her cheeks blooming a bright red that they'd been caught. In a sense, anyway. Whoever had stopped by would see they'd been kissing. The light stubble on his cheeks had rubbed her chin and cheeks, causing a slight redness. The touch of lip gloss she wore was also smeared. He could feel his lips wearing some of it.

He pressed his lips hard against hers one last time, before releasing her hair and standing up. "I'll go see who's at the door."

She sat up, brushing her locks of hair out of the tangled mess he'd put it in.

"You look beautiful. So damn beautiful."

Then he walked out of the room before he poured more of his heart out that she wasn't ready to hear.

He had never believed in love at first sight. Not in a million years. And he couldn't claim he loved her the first time he met her. He hadn't even believed her to be a psychic.

But it hadn't taken long for him to fall under her spell.

He loved her. With his entire heart, body, and soul.

No matter how much she denied it, he'd save her life if it was the last thing he ever did with his own.

He'd die for her.

———

CHARLY BRUSHED her fingers across her lips, still feeling the aftereffects of Breck's lips on hers.

Kissed! Finally. And it had been so much more than she had ever imagined. She knew, because her vision would come true, that his touch everywhere else would light her body on fire. More so than it was now.

She should comb her hair and fix her lip gloss before she joined him downstairs and with whoever had stopped by.

She didn't make it two steps before she heard Breck holler for her. Racing down the stairs, her eyes widened in surprise when she saw Bailey in the foyer, clutching her belly.

"What happened?"

Bailey groaned, her face twisting in pain. "I don't know. But it hurts. It hurts so much."

"I'll drive," Breck commanded as he shoved on his shoes.

Charly grabbed her light-pink coat, not wanting to leave the house in only a tank top—no bra on!—and slipped on a pair of sandals. Anything else would take too long, and the way Bailey kept moaning in pain, they didn't have time for anything else.

Bailey had on a coat, so she didn't hesitate to guide her out of the house by holding her arms. Even if she hadn't, Charly wasn't sure she would've been able to keep her hands to herself. Not when Bailey seemed to be hurting so much.

"Did you call Kade?"

Bailey shook her head as she climbed into the backseat awkwardly. Charly slid in after her. Breck said nothing as he zipped out of the driveway as quickly as he could, the tires spinning.

"I couldn't find my phone. After the third time the pain swept in, I ran to your house as fast as I could."

Not surprising. Bailey was still trying to get used to technology. While she loved it, totally fascinated by it all, she could be a scatterbrain at times, leaving her phone in the oddest places. Charly's phone sat on her nightstand in her bedroom. She didn't think to grab it herself.

Breck must've read her mind because his hand popped up with his phone clutched in it. "Use mine."

She nodded, then spoke when she realized he couldn't see her. "Thank you." Then grimaced. "I don't know his number by heart."

Bailey looked stricken with agony. "I don't either." Then she screamed this time, bending over in pain.

"It's programmed in my phone."

Charly didn't know why that surprised her. He and Kade weren't exactly friends. But she didn't ask why, scrolling through his contacts.

Her hand shook as the ringing droned in her ear.

"What now, detective? Looking to ream into me more for leaving Charly alone."

Interesting. Breck got upset with Kade. She'd seen too much when Breck held her upstairs to focus on everything. It had been a whirlwind of images. If she had paused to remember everything she saw, she would've known he'd gotten upset with Kade.

"It's Charly."

Kade inhaled sharply. "Oh. Why do you have Detective Holstrom's phone? Is everything okay?"

Bailey took that opportunity to scream again.

"Bailey!" Kade cried out. "What's wrong with her?"

"She's going into labor. I imagine it's contractions she's feeling."

"It can't be," Bailey moaned. "They didn't say it would hurt this badly. It's too soon. I have a few more weeks to go."

"I'll meet you at the hospital. Let me talk to Bailey."

She handed over the phone, careful not to touch Bailey's hand as she did so. The ride to the hospital was tense. She wanted to comfort Bailey more than she was, but she also didn't want to risk touching her. Between soft cries of pain, she spoke to Kade until they reached the emergency room doors.

Breck popped out of the car, helping Bailey out, taking the option away from Charly. She couldn't have been more grateful. They disappeared inside the building. Breck found her waiting outside by the vehicle.

"I'll park the car." He hesitated. "Do you want to go with Bailey...or me?"

The good friend in her should go with Bailey. The frightened part of her wanted to go with him.

"I understand, Charly. It's a hospital. Bailey understands too."

But no one should have to understand. By now, at her age, she should be able to deal with her powers. Except she couldn't, and walking into the hospital, touching anything without her gloves—which she also didn't grab—would send her into a tailspin. An overload of her senses always wiped her out. The headaches. Oh, the headaches were the worst.

But Bailey needed her. On the off chance it wasn't

contractions and something was truly wrong, her friend would need her.

"I'll...I'll go with Bailey."

Breck nodded and hopped into the vehicle. She walked through the doors that swished open for her—thankfully, one less thing to touch—and asked a nurse where they'd taken Bailey. She'd waited too long to make her decision, and they had already whisked her friend away. The nurse gave her directions to the maternity ward. Using the sleeve of her jacket, she was able to avoid touching the elevator button and the door to Bailey's room.

Charly was surprised at how fast they got her situated in a room. By the panic in Bailey's eyes, Charly feared it wasn't just contractions.

"Are you family?" a nurse in green scrubs asked before she could go near Bailey's bedside.

"Umm...no."

"Please let her stay," Bailey murmured as another wave of pain swept through.

The nurse nodded then joined the other one in blue scrubs near Bailey's bed where she was hooking up various devices to Bailey. One to monitor Bailey's heart rate and one around her belly to monitor the baby's heart rate.

With tentative steps, she walked to Bailey. The moment Bailey grabbed ahold of her hand, another wave of pain hit. Charly wished she would've stayed outside of the building.

Memories rushed through her. The horrifying moments before the life was snuffed out of Bailey. Bailey's cries mingled with her own.

It took Breck's strong grip to untangle their hands. She turned into his embrace, hiding her face from everyone, even him. His warm, strong arms wrapped her into his safety.

"I forgot," Bailey whispered before moaning again.

Charly felt like a horrible friend for not being there for Bailey. Instead of encouraging words, she hid from everything, unable to lift her head from Breck's chest. To her amazement, he offered the words of inspiration to get Bailey through each bout of pain.

She didn't know how long it had been since they arrived, but Kade burst through the door at some point. Like the coward she was, she still didn't look up or let go of Breck.

Breck's soft voice rumbled, but she didn't pay attention to what he was saying. Then he was guiding her out of the room and out of the building. Somehow, they made it to her house. He helped her remove her coat, then moved her to the couch where he pulled her onto his lap. Her head rested on his shoulder as his arms wrapped around her.

"I've never seen you freeze like that. Are you okay? Talk to me, please."

The way he said it made her think he'd asked her that question several times since the hospital. But she hadn't been able to focus on anything. Her mind kept replaying the same loop over and over.

Large hands around Bailey's throat. The life draining out of her. Her shallow breaths. The weakening of her muscles.

The laughter.

The cruel, cruel chuckle right before nothing but death.

"Charly..." His lips hit the side of her head. "Please, sweetheart..."

That was the third time he'd used that endearment with her. She liked it a little too much.

"I—" She hiccupped before blowing out a sharp breath. "When she..."

He hugged her tighter. "It's okay. Whatever it is. It's okay. What did you see?"

"Her death," she whispered.

She felt Breck let out a long breath, tickling the top of her head.

"I'm sorry you had to see that. I know Bailey wouldn't like knowing that either."

"It was horrible. Of course, I knew she had died. For goodness' sake, she was a ghost a few months ago!" She sat up, one of her hands fisting his shirt. "But, Breck, what he did to her...that's how I will...die. I can't get it out of my head now."

His brows puckered low. "Don't say that. I told you not to talk like that."

"Breck—"

"No!" He smoothed a hand behind her head and down her back. "No, Charly. We won't be arguing about that. I will keep you safe."

He was right, of course. There was no point in arguing when she knew it wouldn't make a difference. He would try, but he would ultimately fail.

"He laughed. Right before she died. Right before the last breath left her body. A short, comical chuckle."

"The man was a monster. He killed multiple women."

Yes, she knew that. They had found the bones of his victims in the walls of Kade's new house across the street from hers.

"It's so odd."

The frown he wore deepened. "What?"

"The way he laughed." She shivered from her other terrifying vision. "Just like the man in my death laughs. Isn't that odd?"

10
_____

HOLSTROM SMILED as he placed a delicate hand on Charly's back. Not quite urging her to move forward but offering a small amount of comfort that he was there, he wasn't going anywhere.

She'd had her moment of panic and shock, wrapped in his arms for a while, and then like a light switch, she bounced off his lap and into the kitchen.

To make pies.

Gone was the melancholy expression. The horror of seeing Bailey's death. Replaced with her bubbly persona that he knew she faked. That wasn't Charly. That was the picture she liked to portray to the world so no one would be the wiser. So no one would see the pain and heartache just below the surface.

She insisted Bailey needed a pie once she delivered her bundle of joy. Since she wasn't sure what kind to make, she made three. One apple pie. One rhubarb pie. And one cherry pie. Loud music, upbeat and peppy, filled the kitchen. He couldn't hold back the smiles when she sang along to a few of them. If he hadn't seen her breakdown minutes ago, he would've never guessed anything was weighing on her mind.

As soon as the pies were baked and sat for a short ten minutes, she ushered them out the door and back to the hospital.

Now stepping off the elevator to the maternity ward, he knew she was regretting the impulse to return. He saw it in each step she took forward. Hence his hand on her back, guiding her, letting her know she wasn't alone.

They found the waiting area after asking one of the nurses at the desk along with an update on Bailey. She was still in labor. That was all the nurse would tell them. Mona and Mason were hanging out in the waiting area.

"Any news? The nurse said she's still in labor. Is she doing okay?" Charly asked more subdued than when she was making the pies.

"Kade texted a little while ago. The baby is in a breech position. They thought the baby would turn on its own, which generally they do by thirty-six weeks. They're preparing to do a C-section." Mason grimaced. "He said Bailey's in a lot of pain. She's having a hard time handling the contractions."

"Well, she's in good hands here," Charly said with a bright smile, the dreariness gone. Then she lifted the containers in her hands. "I made pies!"

Mona brightened at that, standing up from the chair she'd been relaxing in. "I love pie. What kind? Unless we're waiting for Bailey to have some first."

"I made three. There will be plenty to have later."

Charly beelined it to the small counter on the opposite side of the room where they had a pot of coffee and condiments set up. She set the containers down, then proceeded to empty the bag of utensils and plates they brought with as well.

Holstrom didn't miss the way she trembled every time she pulled something out of the bag and set it on the counter. He knew she was being careful about what she touched and how she touched, despite wearing her gloves. The need to be wary was ingrained in her.

Mason moved closer. "Is she okay? Kade mentioned she touched Bailey's hand."

What a loaded question. Was Charly okay? No, he suspected she wasn't. Pretending everything was fine didn't make a person okay.

"She's hanging in there."

He didn't think it was Mason's business to go any further on the matter.

Mona dug into the cherry pie, her eyes lighting up with pleasure with the first bite. Mason asked for a piece of cherry as well, despite not looking too eager for a piece. Holstrom was glad the man didn't argue. Keeping Charly in a good mood and not spiraling back into bleakness was the main goal while they were in the hospital.

He took a piece of apple pie, while Charly cut herself a piece of the rhubarb pie. Everyone ate in silence, enjoying the delicious treat, yet their minds far away and worry settling in their gut.

Charly cleaned everything once she finished with her piece, putting the lid back on the containers.

Silence continued once their plates were emptied. He wanted Charly to take a seat, relax, let her worries dissipate. But he also didn't want to press the issue because he knew her feelings on touching things.

She took the struggle out of the equation for him when

she sat down, her hands resting on her lap, her back ramrod straight, not touching the seat cushion. He sat next to her.

Mona and Mason took that as their cue to sit as well, sitting across from them.

Silence reigned again.

He wasn't an overly talkative guy. More often than not, he remained quiet, taking in his surroundings, weighing, observing, assessing everything before him. But sometimes the lack of noise bothered him.

"Did you have time to close..." Ugh, he hating specifying because it made everything more real. "That issue at Kade's old house." Not to mention, even though they were the only ones in the room, he didn't want to risk any outsider walking by hearing their odd conversation.

Mona smiled while Mason frowned. Complete contrasts of each other, and it did not help to settle the concern in his gut.

"We did, more or less," Mona replied first.

What the hell did that mean?

Perhaps his expression voiced the question that popped into his head because Mason continued. "There was no presence in the area."

"So..." He needed them to dumb it down for him. That didn't make any sense. "Elaborate please."

"Mona conducted the closure spell, and when it was over, no presence could be felt."

Mason was leaving something out, he could tell.

"And before the closure...thing?"

The sudden twinkle in Mona's eyes said she was laughing at him, at his refusal to acknowledge certain words.

"No presence detected then either."

That didn't make any damn sense.

"Something came through that day," he insisted, leaning toward them. "That something nearly pushed Bailey down the stairs. Even Adam, the punk who broke in the other day, said something felt off at the top of the stairs. So what you're saying doesn't add up."

Mona shrugged, biting her bottom lip, then pulled a piece of licorice out of her pocket, chewing ravenously.

Mason sighed, rubbing his chin, though he also remained quiet.

They didn't want to explain what they clearly could not explain.

Charly inhaled sharply, sitting even straighter, which he didn't think was even possible since she had already been ramrod straight.

"Can a spirit attach to another person?" Charly spit the question out so fast, Holstrom had to repeat it in his head a few times.

He hoped the hell not! He'd been half-joking when he mentioned Nathan being possessed.

Mona chomped vigorously on another piece of licorice. "Perhaps."

"Perhaps?" he enunciated slowly. This shit was *not* happening. "What are we talking about here?"

Charly's gloved hand grasped his arm. "Possession, Breck. They didn't sense anything in the beginning because one of those two men who broke in are...possessed."

No.

Nope.

He did not want to have this crazy conversation. It couldn't have happened. It couldn't be real.

"As much as I hate to agree with that, I do agree," Mason stated. "Adam did say his friend Nathan, who you can't currently locate, was acting weird. Not like himself."

"So this Nathan guy is running around with a demon spirit in his body. Controlling him? Is that what you're all saying?"

Because it sounded insane coming out of his mouth.

"I don't think it's a demon," Mona said with a cheery smile, as if now that it was out in the open she didn't have to masquerade her worries.

"Then what is it?" he demanded through gritted teeth.

Charly gasped.

He jerked his attention her way, hating the horror filling her beautiful hazel eyes. Odd how they had been a purple hue when she had a vision and now they were more a golden amber.

"What?" He brushed her cheek with his free hand as she still held his right arm in a death grip. "What is it, sweetheart?"

"I...his laugh...both visions..." She twisted in her seat, her other hand gripping his arm now. He could feel her nails dig into his skin, she had such a latch onto him. "It's him."

"Who, Charly? I don't know what you're trying to tell me."

"The man...who killed...Bailey."

BRECK LOOKED at her as if she'd lost her mind. And part of her felt like she had. The rational part of her had fled a while ago. Nothing but panic and anguish lived inside now.

"You think the man, Thomas, that killed Bailey over a hundred years ago, is possessing Nathan now?"

She nodded, unable to voice it out loud again. Once had been enough for her.

"That makes sense actually."

Charly looked at Mona, wishing she could find a smile to produce as Mona did at the moment. How could she smile at a time like this? Nothing was happy or enjoyable or smile-worthy that they were talking about. She'd used all her bubbly persona to make the pies and deliver them to the hospital. She didn't have it in her to continue that fakeness.

Mona continued, "When we conducted the first two spells at Kade's new house, Thomas could've been near the portals. Bailey's presence at each spell could've pulled him through. We did it three times. The third time was the charm. He jumped through and lingered...until Kade's house was broken into."

"So you're telling me that a psychopathic killer who murdered at least five women that we know about over a hundred years ago," Breck ground out through clenched teeth, noting the four bodies they'd found in Kade's house and Bailey's murder as well, "is now possessing a criminal with a rap sheet a mile long? Is that what you're telling me?"

"Oh my god, Breck."

She couldn't be certain about the idea that popped into her head, but it felt right.

"Nathan is who's going to kill me."

He snapped his attention to her. "Like hell he will. I won't keep saying it. You're not dying this week. And not for a very long time."

She didn't want to argue about that fact. "Don't be bull-headed. Listen to what I'm saying. He's the killer in my vision. He's the one who murdered that woman you're investigating. She was strangled. Bailey was strangled. I will be strangled. Find Nathan and you can..." Could it be possible? "You can stop my vision from happening."

Since she didn't want to argue with him about it, she'd start to have his confidence in the matter.

"That makes sense too," Mona chirped in. "Thomas strangled the women he killed. It would stand to reason whoever he possessed would continue to murder in the same way."

"I hate this conversation," Breck groaned, then he nodded. "But I won't discredit anything you two are saying."

Charly shoved his arm. "Go. Go find Nathan."

"I'm not leaving you alone."

Mason cleared his throat. "Mona can stay with her. I'll go with you. The faster we find this son of a bitch, the better."

Breck frowned. "And when we find him? What about the spirit possessing him? Uh! How do we handle that little problem?"

Mona bit her lip. "We'll need to conduct an exorcism. Or let him stay in Nathan. Nathan killed a woman. Thomas killed several women. Either way, they both deserve to be behind bars."

"This is insane," Breck muttered, shaking his head. "I can't even place Nathan at the crime scene."

"You can't discredit it either. You don't know where he's been." She smoothed one of her hands across his cheek, wishing she didn't have a glove on so she could feel his bristled skin. "You keep saying you can stop my death. Well, here's your chance."

He leaned closer, wrapping his hand behind her neck. His warm hand against her skin sent ripples of pleasure throughout her body. "And if we're wrong and it's not Nathan, if it's some other psycho out there, then what? How am I stopping anything?"

"I can't explain how I know it to be true, but it is. Nathan is your killer. My killer. You and Mason leave. Mona and I will wait here for news on Bailey. I won't leave until you come back or Donnie arrives to bring me home."

His eyes flashed with fire, telling her he didn't like the idea of Donnie coming to her rescue. Oh, the jealousy. If they weren't having such a serious conversation, she'd relish in the idea that he was getting jealous of another man. A vampire, no less.

"You wasted all day with me. It's time to do your job."

He moved closer until his lips were caressing hers. "No time with you is ever wasted. Do not leave this hospital with anyone but me."

Another point she'd like to argue, but tempting fate with this man more than once a day wasn't high on her to-do list. She'd be safe leaving with Mona or Donnie, but nothing would sway his mind.

"And while I'm gone, tell Donnie he's not needed at night anymore." Then his lips were crushing hers and she knew exactly why he wouldn't be needed.

The vision of them having sex would come true tonight.

11

THEY SETTLED INTO HIS CAR, his nerves ramping up to levels he hadn't experienced in a long time. The last time he could remember was getting a phone call from one of his co-workers that they pulled a car out of a lake. That he should come right away.

The entire drive had been laden with anxiety. Knowing the worst news was going to come, no matter how hard he prayed the opposite would happen. Danielle had been found in the driver's seat with her seatbelt still latched. They could only deduce that she couldn't get the belt off or the impact of slamming into the lake knocked her out. Either way, she had drowned.

After it happened came the looks. The unwanted sympathy. The condolences he couldn't handle. It had been his fault she left that night upset. Nobody should be treating him as a distraught partner.

So he moved. For the past seven years, he lived a nice quiet life doing what he did best: solving crimes. Sure, he dated here and there, but he never let another woman in as far as he had with Danielle. The risk had always been too great.

Until Charly.

A throat cleared, jerking him out of his wandering thoughts. Breck looked over at Mason.

"She's going to be okay. She's safe with Mona."

He scoffed internally. Was she though? Mona was the one who'd cast the spell and screwed up letting a psychotic spirit loose in the world.

Instead of responding, because nothing nice would come out of his mouth, he started the car and headed toward Adam's house. He'd start with the easy locations and work his way up to the harder ones.

Adam had nothing new to report. Nathan hadn't been by since they last stopped over or even called him. Breck made Adam try calling him in front of them, and it went unanswered. So obviously Nathan was smart enough not to stay connected with his friends while on a murder spree.

Or should Breck say, Thomas was smart enough? Seemed more appropriate, considering the man got away with murder. Five murders, to be exact. Unlike Nathan whose rap sheet spoke for itself. He was a petty criminal compared to Thomas.

They went down the list of known places Nathan frequented, coming up empty everywhere. The man hadn't been seen by anyone. Which, according to them, was odd. They even visited Javier Capero, the leader of the local gang in town. He had his hands in everything. Drugs, illegal weapons, stolen merchandise. Breck wouldn't be surprised if he had a few officers on his payroll as well.

Even Javier had nothing to share. Of course, Breck couldn't be sure if that was because Javier never shared anything with law enforcement no matter what, or if he truly hadn't seen Nathan.

By eight o'clock, they called it an evening and headed back to the hospital. Mona and Charly were nowhere to be seen. Breck didn't let his heart jump out of his chest yet. They knew Bailey had a successful C-section and mom and baby were both healthy and in recovery. When they found the room where Bailey had been transferred to, it took all his strength not to explode.

"Where's Charly?"

Everyone stared at him as if he'd grown antlers on his head. Was it rude not to inquire how Bailey and the baby were doing? Yes. Did he care? Not at all. Charly was not in the room and that was all he cared about.

Mason sidled up next to Mona who stood by the window. Kade had been sitting in a chair on the opposite side of the bed near the crib where their sweet bundle of joy slept. At Breck's clipped words, Kade stood up.

"Donnie took her home an hour ago."

The anger swelled inside. He told her not to leave without him.

Kade strode toward him in three long strides, getting damn near nose-to-nose with him. "Cool your anger. Now! She had to leave. It was getting to be too much for her."

Not much could lessen his anger when it hit the fan, but those few words did the trick. A strangled breath let loose.

"I'm starting to see you actually have a heart."

Breck narrowed his eyes.

"Not sure I like you directing your affections toward one of the sweetest women I know."

"It's not any of your damn business."

"Seeing as she's my friend," Kade shrugged, "almost like a sister to me, I'm making it my business. Don't hurt her."

"That is the last thing I would ever do. I'm trying to keep her alive while you keep putting her in danger. I should tell *you* not to hurt her."

This time Kade narrowed his eyes. "She's with Donnie."

"A. Damn. Vampire!" Breck annunciated and then snarled the last word.

"Yes, a vampire I would trust with my son's life."

Breck took a step back. "Congratulations on your bundle of joy." Then he walked out of the room before he socked the new dad in the face.

No one ran after him, and honestly, he hadn't expected any of them to do so. They weren't friends. They weren't even acquaintances. They were simply people he had to deal with while working his cases.

When he arrived at Charly's house, he took one step onto the porch before a soft voice from his left spoke.

"If you raise your voice to her, I will raise mine with you."

Breck jerked his attention toward the sound. Donnie emerged from the shadows, his eyes glowing a bright red. In that moment, knowing and believing the man was a vampire merged together.

"You can leave."

The sly smirk Donnie wore said he knew how hard Breck's heart was beating. The anxiety and fear that coursed through his skin. But his words were clear and strong. The vampire wasn't needed here.

"Why are you upset?" Donnie relaxed against the porch railing as if he didn't have a care in the world. Why would he? He was the stronger and more violent of the two.

Breck crossed his arms, attempting to appear as unaffected as him, even though his heartbeat betrayed him every step of the way.

"I won't ask again you. You can leave."

Donnie chuckled. "That's not asking. That's telling me to do something." Donnie shot up so fast and into his face, Breck flinched and stumbled back a step. "I don't take kindly to assholes like you telling me what to do."

The beast before him relaxed again, the damn sly smirk back on his face. "You can be irritated she left the hospital if you'd like, but you will not take that anger out on her. That's a *you* problem. Not a Charly problem. She doesn't answer to you. Now I'll say it one more time, do not raise your voice at her."

Why were they arguing over this? He never had any intention of yelling at Charly. Reprimanding her for disobeying his...Well. Shit. The vampire had a point that Breck hated to admit was right. He didn't have the right to tell her what to do. All these people—vampires included—had been in her life a lot longer than him.

The shit-eating grin Donnie morphed into gnawed at his gut. He wanted to wipe the look off his face. There would be no doing that. He'd never win a fight against a vampire.

"I'm glad we understand each other. Now I will leave you two alone." Donnie turned and jaunted down the two short steps, then twisted his way. "I don't believe I have to say it, but in case you didn't quite understand me. If you hurt her in any way, make her cry in the slightest, I will show you more than just my red eyes." Then his smile for the first time flashed his long pointy teeth that could rip a person to shreds.

One second he was there, and before Breck could blink, he was gone.

Breck shook off the remnants of that disturbing conversation and knocked on Charly's door.

CHARLY'S HAND gripped the wine bottle when the knock echoed throughout the house. She hadn't pulled the cork out yet, so it could be used as a weapon. Then she laughed at herself, setting it on the counter. Donnie would never let her killer knock on the door. It had to be Breck.

When she opened it, they stared at each other for the longest time.

She expected some berating for leaving the hospital with Donnie when he explicitly told her not to. While she had tried her hardest to follow his directions, she failed. Her emotions, her senses had been on overdrive, and she had needed her own space before she fell apart. Even when she saw Bailey and the new baby, the joy she should've felt couldn't be conjured.

"I'm sorry."

She frowned. "For what?"

Breck inhaled deeply, then let it out in a big rush, a chuckle floating out in the end. "I don't know. I want to be mad you left the hospital without me, but I get it. I don't like it, but I get it."

She smiled, grabbed his hand, flinched at the flashes of images, then pulled him inside, closing the door.

"Yeah, I got threatened by a vampire. That's a first."

She squeezed his hand, acknowledging that was what she had seen. "You both care, otherwise you wouldn't get in each other's faces."

His free hand cupped her cheek. "I do care about you. It's kind of scary how much I do in such a short time. That's never happened to me before. I don't know how to process it properly. You're going to have to forgive me quite a few more times in the future."

If she had a future, though she was wise enough not to voice that.

"There's nothing to forgive, Breck. I did leave when you asked me not to. You have a right to your anger."

"It wasn't anger." His mouth lowered. "It was fear."

Then his lips connected with hers and nothing but desire floated between them. Apologies, the rage, the worry...it all dissipated.

But the kiss ended way too soon for her tastes.

"I'm spending the night."

Her face lit up with glee. She already knew this. Thanks to her vision. "Of course."

His brows pleated for a moment as if deciding if he had to decipher her simple response.

"I have a spare bag of clothes in the car for emergencies. I'm going to go grab it. I'd love a shower before..."—he grinned—"we go to bed."

If she hadn't had the vision of them already making love, she'd tell him how presumptuous he was to assume he'd be allowed in her bed.

"I'll pour us some wine. Did you eat? I can heat you up something as well."

"Now that you mention it, Mason and I didn't eat anything."

They went their separate ways. He quickly grabbed his belongings from his vehicle and showered. She opened the wine bottle and poured two generous glasses of wine. If they were having sex tonight, she'd need a little liquid courage. Having done nothing but kiss a man, she knew she would be terrible at it.

Though the vision depicted otherwise. Maybe she wouldn't do so bad after all.

By the time she made him a ham and turkey sandwich

with a side of pita chips and hummus, Breck was finished in the shower. He looked even more dashing in a pair of worn jeans and a black T-shirt.

They took a seat at her kitchen table, silence filling the air while he ate. He took sips of wine here and there, but nothing like the huge gulps she did. When her first glass was nearly empty, she scooted her chair back to refill her glass. His hand covered hers before she could fully stand.

"Don't fill it up again."

She wanted to ask how he knew what her intentions were. But then again, the man was a detective. It didn't take a genius to know what she had been about to do, considering the empty glass was clutched in her other hand.

"Why not?"

He leaned closer, enough to where he was able to reach for the glass and take it away from her, setting it on the table.

"You seem rather nonchalant about me planning to sleep in your bed. No coaxing from me. No arguments. Just acceptance. Which means you know what will happen. Which means you're drinking for courage, and I don't want that."

"Did you forget I'm a...virgin?" *Ugh!* Did they need to have this talk? It was going to happen no matter what.

As that thought rolled around, so did her other vision. The one of her murder.

"Hey," he crooned softly, standing up and pulling her along with him. His arms wound around her, settling firmly on her back. "Why the sudden panic in your eyes? It has nothing to do with us sleeping together. It has nothing to do with the fact you're a virgin, which, I might add, is okay. I would never hurt you. We don't have to do anything you don't want to do."

An empty laugh escaped. "That's the problem, Breck. I already know what's going to happen."

He frowned, but before he could respond, she continued. "The other night when I had a vision..." She shivered at the memory. "It was us making love. I'm not afraid of what's going to happen tonight. It doesn't mean I don't have jitters. It is my first time!"

His hand brushed up her back, scorching her skin as his fingertips caressed upward until he hit her neck. Then they took a soothing path back down.

"Which is why you didn't want to tell me about your vision."

The crooked grin he wore should've had her anxiety lessening and back into pleasure mode, but it didn't.

"Why are you afraid then?"

He always knew how to jump to the heart of the matter.

"I thought I could help prove you're right by stopping a vision before it happened. Yet, here it's happening."

His face puckered into rage, his hands tightened on her back to the point she felt his fingernails dig into her skin. "How many times do I have to tell you I will not let you die?"

She smoothed a hand across his roughened cheek, pressing her lips gently on his. "I know, Breck. I know. It doesn't stop me from panicking that it will happen."

Then her other hand grasped his other cheek, gripping him hard so he wouldn't be able to look away from her. Not that she suspected he would. Because Breck was nothing but honest and unafraid to face anything head-on.

"But if it does happen, you can't blame yourself."

"Charly—"

"No! Promise me right now that you won't blame yourself. You promise me that, and I'll never make another comment about it again."

His words came out in a whisper. "I promise."

It surprised her he relented so quickly about the matter. But then again, the man was as stubborn as her. He had to figure it was easier to accept her words than fight her on it.

"Now we'll never speak of that again." His lips brushed against hers. "On to the other issue at hand."

She ran her fingers through his hair, delighted at the sigh that left his mouth. "That is?"

"We are going to bed right now, aren't we? You know what's going to happen, and it's not fair I don't. So I want to see it for myself now."

She giggled when he lowered his mouth and smothered her with kisses on the neck. "Yes, Breck, let's go to bed now."

"Good. While I'm loving your body up and down, I'll be sure to prove your vision wrong and do things that you never saw coming."

She couldn't wait for him to prove her wrong.

12

HE'D EATEN MOST of the sandwich she made, but barely touched his glass of wine. He had no intention of doing so either. Not when he had other more pressing matters at hand. Like getting the most gorgeous woman on the planet naked and under his body.

"We'll clean up tomorrow."

Before she could protest, he pulled her to follow him. There wasn't much resistance on her part, though a low chuckle split the air when he saw her glance at the table as if leaving the mess bothered her.

Once in her room, he closed the door behind them and then locked it. One could never be too careful. Sure, they had two more full days before Friday arrived, but it didn't mean things couldn't change. Her vision told her Friday was circled as the day of her death. But was it? She could've circled Friday for any number of reasons. Honestly, it was a guess on her part.

But none of that mattered. The only thing he wanted on his mind was Charly's undying attention and making sure he pleasured her from head to toe.

They stood by the bed, and he could see the question in her eyes. Why did he lock the door? But he also saw she answered her own question by the flash of awareness right after.

He brushed his hands up and down her arms, loving the softness and the way she trembled at his touch. The way her eyes lit up with bliss and the want for more.

She bit her bottom lip, portraying she was nervous, something she had also admitted. The way his heart beat erratically said he was damn nervous himself. He wanted every second between them to be perfect. He didn't want to disappoint her in the slightest.

He blew out a breath, chuckling. "We're up here now and I'm as nervous as you."

Her sweet laughter mixed with his, lessening the worry coating his gut.

"I trust you, Breck." Her hands touched his chest as she leaned forward, closer to him. "In everything. Since I don't know what I should do, I'm going to let you lead. I sense you like being in charge."

Yeah, he could safely say he didn't like being bossed around.

But with Charly...

In the bedroom...

Well, he wouldn't be opposed to her telling him what to do.

Not that he thought they were ready for that. She was way more anxious than him.

He responded to her honest words by kissing her lips, growling in approval at her happy sigh. His hands found the hem of her tank top, and without missing a beat while kissing her, he had it up and over her head. As soon as the garment hit the floor, she disengaged, her cheeks flushing bright red. That beautiful bottom lip of hers was attacked by her teeth once more.

If she was embarrassed to be naked in front of him, she shouldn't have pulled away. Because now he could gawk. His gaze devoured her pert breasts waiting for him to explore. He loved that she never wore a bra around the house.

Before she could say anything, he cupped her left breast, kneading, caressing, and then tweaking her nipple until a breathy moan slipped out of her. "You're beautiful, Charly."

A shy smile appeared, and then she brushed a hand down his chest. "And you have too many clothes on."

He chuckled, but before he could unbutton his shirt, she started the task for him. He stroked and caressed her breasts, watching as she flicked each button open with trembling hands. Down the line she went, her hands getting steadier the farther she got. Then his shirt fell to the floor.

"Lay down for me."

She nodded, listening without hesitation. It made him wonder how much he could get away with. Not that he was overly rough during sex and liked to be dominating or anything. Kink wasn't his thing. But he loved how she verbalized she trusted him and also showed him by her actions. He treasured her trust like nothing he ever had before.

He divested himself of his pants and boxers, pausing before climbing on the bed. Her eyes bulged and lowered to his cock that wouldn't be able to hold back for long. It was hard and aching.

Maybe he went too fast. The slight fear in her eyes had the worry re-entering his gut. Damn, but this wasn't the perfection he had been going for.

"I'll go slow."

"I'm...not worried."

He couldn't help the low chuckle that slipped out at her tentative words, but it was the smile on her face that had the laughter rising to the surface.

"You look a bit worried."

"I..." her head turned slightly, averting her eyes. "I didn't realize you'd be so..."

His hand couldn't help but cup his cock at her timid words. "So big?"

Her gaze darted back to his, then glided down until she landed on him fondling himself. "Yes."

The breathy way she said it had him increasing the strokes. "God, I want you, Charly. You can take off your pants." He rounded the bed so he could grab a condom from his bag on the chair in the corner. "Unless you want me to do it." He'd be more than happy to perform the task.

Her wily smirk had him cupping his cock again and stroking it a few more times. Then she removed her pants and underwear, tossing them to the floor. He couldn't find the condom fast enough.

He stalked to the bed, climbing on it like a predator about to pounce on its prey.

Then his lips met hers. The kiss was as sweet and potent as all the others. His hand found a breast, stroking and tweaking her nipples until he felt her arch her back. Oh, she was ready for more.

His lips left her mouth, making a path down her neck, pebbling light, feathery kisses along the way. The trail landed at her breasts. He kissed them as thoroughly as his hands had loved them earlier. Charly's tiny cries of pleasure urged him on. Strokes of his tongue on her nipple, then a little bite before soothing it with another kiss. He could stay here all day doing nothing but loving her breasts. But he had more to explore.

His lips continued in their exploration, placing light kisses on her stomach, his tongue dipping into her belly button, eliciting a giggle. His hands gripped her waist as his mouth trailed to her thighs, peppering kisses up and down. Then he hit the spot he'd been craving. She sucked in a sharp breath the moment his lips touched her very core. A few light kisses to get her used to the idea, then his tongue dove in as he licked and played, ringing every ounce of pleasure he could out of her.

Her hands found his head, her fingers digging in. The pressure he felt, the low moans that sailed through the room, only had him licking and sucking more urgently until the blessed crescendo hit.

She cried out his name.

She came too soon. He'd barely begun.

He didn't stop kissing her down there until he felt a tug on his hair.

His head popped up with a crooked grin on his lips. "I was having fun."

The bliss in her eyes made his heart swell with something akin to love. But damn it. It was too soon to love her. They'd barely known each other that long. He didn't believe in love at first sight, so he couldn't fall in love so quickly. Yet his heart at every sweet moment like this told him that he was in love. How could he deny it? Even to himself.

Shrugging that emotion away, he slid up her body, nuzzling her neck, peppering more kisses along the curve until he found her ear and nibbled before kissing her on the lips.

"Can I put the condom on?"

Hell, yes!

He damn near shot up like a rocket and sat back on his knees, holding out the package. Tiny giggles erupted as she sat up as well, eyeing the tiny thing, then her gaze darted to his large cock.

She bit her lip and tore open the package. Thinking she'd slide it on, she surprised him when her hand curled around him first, tentative strokes up and down.

He closed his eyes, breathing heavily. "Oh, God, Charly. You can't do that long. I won't last, sweetheart."

"But you had fun with me, I want some fun too."

Just like with the buttons, she was timid at first. The more she stroked him, the firmer her grip got and the faster she pumped.

His hips moved with her ministrations, the ecstasy building to the point he wanted to come. His eyes popped open as he snatched her hand in a strong grip. "You can play later. But right now, I need to be inside you."

She nodded again, her eyes dilating with an inferno of pleasure. Her hands were confident when the condom went on. He adored that she got over her timidity easily.

He moved forward, causing her to lay back down, and then he was hovering above her. "I promise I'll go slow."

"You won't hurt me, Breck. You can go as fast as you'd like."

Because she knew from the vision? Or because she simply trusted him?

He wasn't going to ask.

Instead, he positioned himself and slowly entered her. The delight that filled every facet of his body was almost too much to bear. He knew he wouldn't last long. It was a damn good thing he packed more than one condom in his spare bag. It might be in his trunk for work emergencies— getting dirty at a crime scene—but a man could never be too prepared. Anything could happen. Like now. With Charly.

As he pumped in and out with a slowness he usually didn't display, he watched as her eyes dilated with pleasure even more than before. Those tiny cries she loved expressing returned. His movements increased. A little faster. A little harder. When she wrapped her legs around his waist, he knew she wasn't afraid of anything happening between them. She had no need to be nervous because she was doing everything perfectly right.

The thrusting increased. His eyes never left hers. They watched each other enjoying the magic being created.

"I'm so damn close, Charly." He closed his eyes, willing himself to hold off. He wanted her to come again. He wanted to feel her tense around him, increasing his own joy.

When he got himself a semblance under control, his eyes re-opened. She still stared at him with wonder and excitement. One of his hands was resting near her head. He snaked that hand into her hair, gripping it as if, if he didn't, she'd slip away from him. The other hand went lower, caressing, stroking, until he found the right spot on her body so she'd scream his name again.

Her fingernails dug into his thighs, and he knew he found the magic spot.

"Oh, yes, Breck. So close too."

He thrusted and pumped, rubbed and stroked until her beautiful lips cried out his name again. There was no need to wait any longer, he growled her name in unison as they both hit the pinnacle.

Spent and elated, he lowered gently until he was lying on her, his mouth close to her neck. A few feather-light kisses hit her before he brushed his hand across her cheek, signifying he wanted her to look at him.

She obeyed.

He smiled before kissing her once. Her return smile filled his heart with even more emotion that he didn't want to acknowledge. Not yet.

"So that was a pretty intense vision you had."

She wound her arm around his back, stroking her hand up and down. "It was."

He wished she had elaborated because he was forced to ask, even though he should let it go.

"And it was exactly as you saw it?"

"A few things were different."

He knew it!

A vision could change.

Though he didn't voice it as he was one never to gloat.

He brushed her cheek again, a sly grin emerging. "Well, now I need to know which parts were different."

She produced her own wily smirk. "Why don't I show you instead?"

And she proceeded to do just that.

SHE GROANED, curling into her side when she heard an alarm go off. Since she didn't use alarms, she knew it was Breck's. The thought that he had to leave sent her into a moment of panic. Her body tensed, thinking of being alone all day and not soaking up every morsel she could with him.

Before she died.

Then a warm hand slid around her stomach, pulling her closer. Her body was tucked nicely into the curve of his. The tension released.

A light kiss hit her neck. She didn't open her eyes, but her lips curled up into a sweet smile. To be touched. To be kissed. To be held by someone was more than she could've ever hoped for. She never wanted to leave this bed.

"Good morning," Breck rumbled in a sleepy tone.

"No, it's not time to get up."

He chuckled, nuzzling her neck and peppering tiny kisses along the curve of her shoulder. "Oh, is my beloved Charly not a morning person?"

She reveled in the fact she was his beloved Charly. The little endearments he parted with on occasion were moments to treasure. No one—no man—had ever spoken to her so romantically. Since Breck didn't seem like the romantic kind of guy, it made his words that much more delightful.

She twisted around, snatching a kiss. "I haven't been sleeping well the last few weeks. I'm usually up before this time. I don't want you to leave."

The happiness in his eyes died. "I have to. Two more days until Friday and I..." His arms around her tightened, his fingertips digging into her back. "I have to find Nathan. Before he hurts anyone else."

That was very true. Nathan could take another victim before Friday. She certainly didn't want that to happen.

"I know you do. It's nice waking up next to someone. To you."

"Well, we'll do it again tomorrow. And the next day." He paused, his entire body taut with tension and his lips in a determined line. "And the next day. And the next day. As many days as you want to wake up next to me."

They were both silent. Her, because she knew he didn't want her to repeat she wouldn't be here past Friday. And him, because he wouldn't argue about it anyway.

"Why don't you get in the shower while I make you

breakfast?" She kissed him and then tried to turn and wiggle out of his embrace. His arms were impenetrable.

"Why don't you shower with me and I skip breakfast?"

His silky smile had her nodding, because who was she to argue with such logic. And any time she could soak up with him she would. Time was precious....and slowly running out.

They scrambled out of bed, the icky tension from before gone. They were already naked. Neither one put any clothes on last night after making love several times. They had to get creative with their pleasure since he'd only had two condoms in his bag. Charly would have to make a store run to buy another box. She imagined Breck wouldn't have an issue with that.

The hot water soothed her achy bones from all the exertion from last night, and Breck's hands scorched the rest of her body with his possessive touch.

Despite neither brushing their teeth yet, they kissed. Nothing slow and tender, but needy and desperate as if they both knew these moments would soon be over. He'd never admit it, but he had to know her vision could come true. With the way he clung to her, his hands roaming but firm, his kisses deep and thorough, he knew it might be one of the last times he held her.

They lathered their hands with soap, stroking each other in every nook and cranny. She'd never had such an erotic shower in her life. Like in bed when she didn't want to leave, she never wanted to leave this shower.

She gripped his cock tight, caressing up and down until a guttural grown filled the tiny space. His hand found her spot, and they loved each other, the shower filling up with steam. Not just from the hot water hitting their skin.

The pleasure rose to the point where she knew she was on the precipice.

"Yes, come for me, Charly. Let go," he whispered in her ear, holding her close.

Her hand went slack for a moment, stroking him when the waves of ecstasy hit her. He held her upright, his strong hold never faltering. Then she resumed pumping his thick cock, until it was her turn to grip him tightly in her arms. He growled in appreciation, his hips pumping in tune with her hand until every last morsel shot out of his body.

Giggles and smiles continued as they washed their hair and then exited the shower. With a towel wrapped around her, she left the bathroom to get dressed. He'd hung his clothes up last night in the bathroom.

The door to the bathroom was still closed after she donned a tank top and a pair of pink shorts. No bra because she knew he enjoyed that. Plus, she had no intention of leaving the house yet, so why wear a bra.

The coffee was halfway through its brewing process when he joined her in the kitchen. He snuck another kiss before grabbing a mug from the cupboard.

"I'll check in with you over the course of the day, but you should be fine with my brother."

She swiveled around, her forehead pleated in confusion. "I'm sorry, what?"

"I called my brother to hang out with you for the day. Kade's with Bailey. Obviously, I'm not that much of a jerk to insist he be with you when Bailey needs him right now." He coughed uncomfortably. "Your night friends can't be here during the day. I'm not asking Mona to come over. She's weird. Same goes for Mason. So that leaves my brother."

"That you rarely speak to?"

He shrugged. "We're not estranged. I'd help him if he

asked. He knows that. We don't get together as often as we should. It's not a big deal."

To Breck it wasn't. To her, it would be extremely uncomfortable.

"I'll be fine by myself. He doesn't need to come."

Breck set his coffee mug down before gripping her hips and pulling her close. "We're not arguing about this. He's on his way. I will not leave you alone." He brushed a lock of wet hair behind her ear. "Please, Charly, don't argue with me about this."

"There's a lot I'm not allowed to argue about with you. It's not fair. You can't tell me what to do, Breck. That's not how this relationship works."

A silky grin grew on his face.

"Why are you smiling?"

"Because you referred to us as having a relationship. We're making headway on your thinking and realizing there will be more between us past Friday."

Well, that's certainly not what she had meant, but she wouldn't specify as she didn't want to wipe the delectable smile off his face. She truly loved when he smiled, something he didn't do nearly enough.

"And what did you tell your brother?"

"The truth. That a psycho has his eyes set on you and you can't be alone."

She doubted he shared the whole truth.

"And that I'm a psychic? That Nathan is possessed by a dead spirit who murdered women over a hundred years ago?"

He winced. "Most of the truth."

She shook her head, laughing, then snuck out of his embrace. "I don't like people in my space. You know why. But I'll let it slide for today. So you don't worry about me."

She grabbed his mug and poured the coffee in it, then handed it to him. "I'll make breakfast while we wait for him."

Breck surprisingly didn't say anything as he rounded the island and took a seat at the counter.

Silence seemed to be the way to go. She bustled around the kitchen making eggs, bacon, and toast. By the time she'd finished, her doorbell went off.

13

BRECK OPENED the door to his brother who wore a goofy-ass grin. Nothing new there. His brother always smiled. It drove him up the wall how he could be so happy and carefree all the time.

"What's up, bro?" Jock slapped him on the shoulder, nodding as he surveyed his surroundings. "Love the aesthetics. Pink is my color."

Breck rolled his eyes as Jock gazed at Charly's couch, a sappy, doe-eyed look that said he couldn't wait to lounge on the pink item. No doubt Jock even had a few pink shirts in his closet. He wasn't saying it for shits and giggles. He, on the other hand, wouldn't be caught dead in anything pink.

"Come on, I'll introduce you to Charly."

Charly stood on the opposite side of the counter, obviously not wanting to get too close to his brother. He understood. He didn't want Jock touching her either.

"Charly, this is my brother Jock. And vice versa. That's Charly."

"So nice to meet you, Charly." Jock wasn't shy in any

aspect of life. He rounded the corner and got in her face, holding out his hand.

Charly stared at his hand, then smiled. "You too. I don't shake hands. I hope you don't mind."

Jock shrugged as if it were a normal thing people said all the time and dropped his hand, getting the hint she wanted her space. He even returned to his original spot next to him. His brother could be cheery to the point it made Breck want to puke, but he wasn't an idiot. He understood subtle clues.

Then Charly giggled. "I love your name."

Jock beamed with pride. "Thanks. I know it's an odd one. At least it didn't turn out to be Jeck."

Breck couldn't help but laugh at that. "That's because Mom filled out your birth certificate instead of Dad. There was no way she'd make a mistake. Only I got that luxury."

"I like the name Breck. It suits you," Charly added.

He knew Charly wasn't one to lie and say things for the hell of it, so he knew she meant every word. He'd gotten used to his name. It didn't bother him like it had as a kid. These days, most people called him Holstrom or detective. Charly was one of the few who used his first name.

"You have a sister too. What's her name? Now I need to know."

Jock propped a leg to the bottom of the chair bar, leaning on the back of the stool. "She got lucky. It's Lucy."

Another sweet giggle erupted from her. "That is a pretty name."

"She's the baby of the family, so she's always been spoiled." Breck said it in a way that he wasn't jealous of the fact.

"You'll have to meet her. She'll love you." Jock shot him a shit-eating grin that he didn't want to decipher. Probably the fact that he rarely dated, and when he did, the women did not meet his family. Not even Danielle had.

Then Jock shot Charly another splendid look, his smile wavering for the first time since entering her house. She wore a melancholy expression, most likely because she was thinking of her vision and her impending death he planned to thwart.

"I said something wrong. I do that sometimes. Put my foot in my mouth," Jock said with a short chuckle. "I assumed you were Breck's girlfriend as he rarely calls me to help out with something of this nature. If it was officially police related, they'd put you in protective custody." Then his gaze swung back to him. "What am I missing, bro?"

He didn't want to get into it. The less Jock knew, the better. Plus, he wouldn't even believe half the stuff he'd tell him. He still had a hard time believing half the shit and he'd seen it with his own eyes.

Charly spoke before he could.

"I'm a psychic. I've had a vision of my death. Breck's being overly cautious."

Jock's brows shot up.

It was moments like this he wished he could find his words faster. He took his time thinking too much before speaking. He hadn't wanted Charly to admit any of that to Jock.

"Rightly so, I'd say."

Damn Jock for being the considerate asshole he always was. Not questioning anything, taking people's word at face value.

"She is my girlfriend," Breck snapped, not sure why he decided after his long moment of silence to start with that.

Another damn shit-eating grin punctured Jock's annoying face.

"And I will do anything and everything in my power to keep you safe, Charly. That isn't being overly cautious, that's just being smart." He realized his tone was too severe when she cringed and wrapped her arms around her middle as if warding him off.

His shoulders slumped as he looked chagrined. "I didn't mean to imply you're dumb. That's not what I meant."

She nodded, her eyes gathering water.

Damn it!

She couldn't cry. Not because of him. Not in front of his brother.

He rounded the counter, clutching her shoulders, then loosening his grip as he slid his hands down her arms and untangled them so he could hold her hands.

"I'm sorry. Please forgive my idiocy."

"I'm not mad at you."

He leaned in closer so Jock couldn't hear a word. "You're about to cry because of me."

"Not because I'm mad."

Wrinkles must've dotted his forehead as he frowned, because she let go of one of his hands and reached up to smooth them out.

"I've never had anyone care so much about me. I know my parents loved me, but..." She sighed heavily as she brushed her hand through his wet hair. "They kept their distance. They were afraid to touch me. It doesn't seem to scare you. You can't keep your hands off me now. I'm not used to that, Breck. I'm not used to someone being...being here for me."

"And it's never going to change. Now that I know how you feel in my arms, I can't seem to get enough." He kissed her softly, relishing in the feathery sigh she released. "My brother will get on your nerves with his cheeriness, but he'll keep you safe. He won't let anyone hurt you."

Her whole face lit up with delight. "Cheeriness doesn't frighten me. I exude bubbliness like it's my only personality. I like your brother. He's the complete opposite of you."

That last statement had his heart skipping a beat. What the hell did that mean? She liked Jock more than him? Was he too stern and unfeeling for her?

Her hand caressed his cheek, tracing his lips that had fallen into another frown. Then she brushed her tender hand to his forehead, smoothing those wrinkles out again.

"That sounded wrong. I'm sorry. I like the grumpiness in you. Don't change, Breck."

He heard the unspoken words as well: Don't be jealous.

"I should go before I decide I can't leave you."

"We'll be fine."

He had no doubt about that. If she already liked Jock in the short amount of time she'd been in his company, they'd be best buddies by the time he came back. That's just how Jock operated. He got everyone to like him, while Breck always pushed people away. The jealousy started to worm its way to his heart. He had to leave before it took permanent residence.

He kissed her one more time before backing away and stopping in front of Jock. "Don't touch her. I don't say that as a warning because she's my girlfriend. I say it because if you do, she'll see things you don't want her to see."

Jock's brow rose at that, looking at him, then glancing at Charly. "What things?"

She grinned. "Every kind of thing. I'm a psychic, remember?"

"You were touching her."

Breck nodded. "Yeah, because I have nothing to hide

from her. Because I like touching her and I had to get the hard part over with. I'm advising you that if you touch her, you might not like what happens."

Jock's mouth widened into a sly grin again. "And she's your girlfriend and you don't want anyone touching her, even your brother. I hear you, bro."

"Yeah, that too," he snapped. Jock knew how to get under his skin with ease. He hated it.

"I'll check in later. I—" He froze, nearly letting the words I love you slip out. "I hope you have a pleasant day with this idiot."

Then he turned and stalked out of the room before those elusive words came out anyway.

Love?

So soon?

It couldn't be possible, yet with everything that had happened in the last week, it shouldn't surprise him.

But it did.

He'd fallen in love with a woman who, if he didn't stop it, would die in a few days.

CHARLY LOOKED AROUND THE ROOM, anywhere but at Jock. Awkward didn't even begin to describe how she felt. Breck leaving so abruptly. Being stuck with a man she didn't know.

She shivered.

Wearing not much clothes with no bra on. That had to be rectified immediately.

"Umm...help yourself to the food. I'm going to change."

Then she vacated the kitchen as fast as Breck had.

She took her time putting on a bra and a large T-shirt that she didn't mind getting dirty—and that would hide her assets. Her shorts were swapped for pants. Once dressed, she felt a little better.

Jock was chomping on the breakfast she had made, pointing enthusiastically at it when she entered the kitchen.

"Crispy bacon is my jam. You did a great job. I will be having seconds if you don't mind."

"Please, have as much as you'd like."

She cleaned up as he ate, a comfortable silence filling the room, surprisingly, since she had left the kitchen feeling off-kilter in front of him.

When Jock was finished and she had added his plate to the dishwasher, she smiled in his direction, the nerves back with a vengeance. She liked it better when he was occupied with something and not his full attention on her.

"So, what do you do, Jock? I hope you're not missing anything important because of me."

"It's my day off. I'm a firefighter."

"You both went into a profession that helps people. I like that."

Jock nodded. "I love my job. Keeps me active and in shape. I meet a lot of interesting people. And like you said, I help people. I enjoy doing that."

He stood up from the stool. "What's on the agenda today? Anything you need help with."

"I hope you don't mind I work in my shed. I have a client who wants a bench. I haven't started it yet. It would be helpful if you help with the wood and cutting. Sometimes, those pieces can get heavy."

Jock flexed, grinning. "I'm the man for the job. Let's do this!"

They ventured outside, getting to work right away. At times, they were silent, and at other times, Jock made small talk. Eventually, she got comfortable around him as if he'd been a part of her life for years. He made it very easy to like him. Cracking jokes, making her laugh at silly things. Being constantly upbeat and positive. So strange how Breck was the opposite.

They'd just finished a ham sandwich with a side salad when her doorbell went off.

Jock stood up so fast from his chair, his body rigid, she saw the similarities to Breck right away. When it came to her safety, neither man played around.

"Expecting company?"

"No, but I do have visitors on occasion. The mailman knocks on the door sometimes when my packages are too large for the mailbox. Kade could be stopping by to check on me, even with Bailey in the hospital. It doesn't necessarily mean it's someone bad. Would a killer ring the doorbell?"

He gave her a crooked grin, chuckling. "You make a good point. Even so, stay here while I check it out."

Throughout the morning, they'd also broached the subject of her impending death. The people close in her life who'd been helping her stay safe. She even mentioned Donnie and the other vampires, though left out the part where they were blood-sucking creatures. He'd taken her being a psychic pretty well. She didn't want to push her luck with vampires, or the fact Bailey had been a ghost until recently.

When she heard the soft, feminine voice float to the kitchen, she made her way to the foyer.

"Mona, I didn't expect to see you."

She knew Breck wouldn't be happy about her visit. While she didn't agree with him that Mona was weird, she didn't connect with her as well as she did with Bailey.

"I hope you don't mind. I thought you could use a friend."

She waved her in, nodding at Jock that it was okay. Her eyes widened when Scatter and Bozo strolled in after her.

"Is that a wolf?" Jock asked, stepping back a few steps.

Mona stroked the top of Bozo's head, smiling. "He's friendly. You don't need to worry." Then Mona held out her hand. "I'm Mona. And you are?"

Jock shook her hand. "Jock, Breck's brother."

Mona pulled a piece of licorice out of her sweater pocket, nibbling before replying. "I had no idea he had a brother. Nice to meet you."

"He has a sister too." Charly didn't know why she added that. Maybe to keep up the conversation, even as stilted and awkward as it was.

"Licorice?" Mona asked, holding out another piece toward Jock.

"Yeah, why not." He bit into it merrily, making Charly giggle under her breath. The man rolled with the punches. Not much seemed to faze him.

Mona held one out to her, but she declined with a quick shake of her head. Even though it was food, she could still get a residual reading from Mona because she was touching it.

Meow.

Scatter meandered down the hallway toward the kitchen.

"Scatter likes your house. He hopes you don't mind he explores."

Being good friends with Kade and Bailey, Charly was around Mona and Mason quite often when they ventured to Kade's house. Scatter and Bozo usually tagged along. It didn't make it any easier to get used to the fact Mona and

Mason could understand the animals as if they spoke the human language.

"Of course. Both of them are welcome to go wherever they want."

Jock frowned but said nothing.

What did you say to someone when they acted like their cat could speak?

"I didn't come empty-handed." Mona lifted a large black pouch that Charly had seen her carry often. Usually, potions were hidden inside.

Mona bit her bottom lip. "I thought I'd add a protective spell around the house. To keep unwanted spirits and bad energy out."

Jock cleared his throat. "A spell?"

Charly giggled. Oh, poor Jock. He was about to get another lesson in the paranormal world. Because how could she keep the truth from him? She wasn't about to lie.

"Mona's a witch."

At the sound of her name, she sent Jock a brilliant smile, nibbling away at her candy.

"Okay. And the animals can speak." Jock pointed at her. "You're a psychic. What else am I missing?"

When in Rome...

"Well, the killer is presumably possessed by an evil spirit who killed several women over a hundred years ago. He's back killing more women in the same way. He killed Bailey back then, and she lived in the house across the street as a ghost until Kade moved in and she somehow turned human again." Charly widened her hopeful smile, hoping he wouldn't lose his mind after that confession. "Oh, and vampires exist. Donnie watches my house at night. He's a sweetheart."

"Isn't he though?" Mona chirped. "You can always count on Donnie and the boys."

"I feel like Breck left out a lot of information when he called me this morning."

"He is a man of few words." That was all Charly could think to say. Because, honestly, what else could she say?

Mona lifted her magic bag. "So, shall we chant some spells and sprinkle some potion around this joint?"

14

HE'D STOPPED by the precinct to grab Carla's file, something he should've had on his person to begin with. He regretted the decision when he saw the last person he wanted to see stroll into the room.

"Can I help you?"

Mason chuckled. "I'm here to help you. You didn't answer my call earlier. I thought I'd swing by anyway."

"Don't you have something else to do? I'm good." Holstrom stood up, hoping Mason would take the hint and leave. Either way, he was leaving as well. He had a killer to find.

"Why do you do that?"

Holstrom cocked a brow. No need for him to ask what Mason was talking about. He knew. Why did he push people away? Why did he have a hard time accepting help? Why was he an asshole?

Because.

Though he wouldn't give that answer because it never satisfied people—it wouldn't for Mason—and he knew it pissed everyone off as well. He didn't go out of his way to upset others. It just happened.

"If there's nothing else, I'll be on my way."

Then he strolled past Mason as if he hadn't rejected his offer of help and acted like a colossal ass.

Mason wasn't one to get the hint. He followed Holstrom to his car.

"You didn't seem to have an issue with me yesterday when I tagged along. Why now?"

He clutched the doorframe of his vehicle, letting out a breath before responding. "I never said I didn't have an issue yesterday. I caved in, despite my reservations about you. Need I remind you this problem I have right now, this killer I'm trying to find, is because of your girlfriend. Excuse me if I don't trust you."

Mason had the decency to look remorseful. "I will admit that Mona is still learning at..." He paused as if struggling with finding the right words. "You're going to stand here in front of me and tell me you've never made mistakes. Mistakes that had serious consequences. Is that what you're telling me? That you're Mr. Perfect!"

His fingers tightened on the frame, the metal digging into his skin. The pain felt good. For a second it masked the pain in his heart.

He would never say he was perfect. Or didn't make mistakes. If he hadn't crushed Danielle's heart on a stormy night, maybe she'd still be alive today. But he had and she died. That had been a grave mistake on his part.

It didn't mean he wanted to continue being around these...freaks. That was the nicest word he could think of.

If he was being honest with himself, it was their fault Charly had a vision of her death. If Mona hadn't performed the spell in Kade's old house, Thomas's spirit would've never slipped through and stayed. He would've never possessed

Nathan. And Charly wouldn't be on a serial killer's list to die.

So yeah, he didn't want to be around them, even if Mason wanted to help find a demonic spirit causing havoc in town.

"Silence will not make me walk away. You need my help, even if you don't want to admit it."

Holstrom clenched his jaw, refusing to utter any sort of truth to that statement. Maybe he did need his help, at least once he caught Nathan. Did they perform an exorcism? Did they lock Nathan up possessed? He had no idea what he'd do, and Mason knew it.

"Whatever. I don't have time for this shit. Follow me if you like, but I'm not riding with you today."

While that might've seemed petty of him, he didn't care one iota.

Mason did as he suggested and followed him to Carla's apartment building where he interviewed her neighbors again. Mason popped in with a few questions of his own. Nothing had changed, and he hadn't expected anything to. It was just what he did. He revisited, reinterviewed until that one tiny thing popped out and helped him break a case wide open.

Before sliding into his vehicle, he caught sight of the yoga studio. It wouldn't hurt to chat with them again. It was a different woman behind the desk when he walked in. She had short, spiky blonde hair and a friendly smile. He introduced himself, begrudgingly introduced Mason, and asked the same questions he'd asked the previous woman. Nothing new again.

Then he asked a brand new question that he should've asked the first time.

"Do you have surveillance cameras outside?"

The studio was directly across the street from Carla's apartment. Any kind of video could be helpful. He wouldn't know unless he checked it out.

"We do. I don't see how that's helpful though. Our cameras don't point all the way to the apartment buildings."

"You never know what might be helpful. Do you mind if we have a look at the videos from Tuesday? The early-morning hours?"

She shrugged and waved them back behind the counter to a room that looked like an office. It also had a tiny space set up in the corner with a yoga mat, weights, and a mirror. She fiddled with the computer, then gestured for him to take a seat. He sat down while Mason stood behind him. She left the room while they searched.

When he started the video for last Tuesday at around midnight, it showed the parking lot for the yoga studio and part of the road. At that time of night, there wouldn't be much traffic. Maybe he'd get lucky and see Nathan driving into the complex.

Around 12:43 AM, he stopped the video and rewound it, playing it again when a dark-blue truck turned into the complex. A few other vehicles had driven by, but none had turned into the complex.

The truck was coming from the direction where it turned right into the complex, so the driver's side was in view of the camera. It was dark out though. Hell, it was the middle of the night, of course the lighting would be terrible.

He paused the video, zooming in as best as he could, though it got blurrier the larger the picture became.

"It's too dark to say if that's a man or woman," Mason pointed out, leaning toward the video.

"It's the first vehicle to turn into the parking lot."

He rewound the video again to catch the license plate

number. That was also hard to see, but he managed to make out most of it.

They continued watching the video, stopping it again at 1:21 AM when a car this time pulled into the complex. Again turning right, giving them a view of the driver's side. Still too dark to make out who was driving, but enough of an angle to get a license plate.

After viewing more of the footage until well past 4 AM, Holstrom's heart sank. Neither vehicle that had pulled into the parking lot had left in that timeframe. Meaning it was mostly likely residents of the building who had gone home for the evening. Not a serial killer out to rape and murder an innocent woman and then leaving after doing the deed.

Regardless, he took the little information he had, thanked the woman, and left. He left his car door open while he plugged the information into the police database from the computer he carried around. The truck was registered to Tony Anderson who lived in the complex. Not his killer. The car, however, was registered to Mary Johnson, who had reported her vehicle stolen last Monday evening.

"Well, holy shit," Mason muttered, then glanced across the street to the parking lot. "That could've been him. He left the vehicle there."

Mason retreated to his car while Holstrom started his up and went back across the street. They found the car parked in the far back of the lot, the doors unlocked and the keys on the floor of the passenger seat.

"I'll call a crime scene crew to test for prints and what-not." Holstrom made the call, making it sound urgent. Which it was. The sooner they found Nathan, the more the weight on his shoulders would decrease.

It took them over an hour to arrive, and Holstrom tried not to express his annoyance. He knew he failed. He left the vehicle in their capable hands, reminded them to call him immediately with any news, and headed to Mary Johnson's house.

It might be another dead end.

But it also could be another good lead to finding his killer.

———

CHARLY SAT on the couch with a cup of coffee, sipping it, more so to hide the smile she wore. Every time she glanced at Jock, he had a look of terror on his face. She couldn't tease him for it because every time she looked at Mona she wore the same expression as him. But on him, the look was too adorable. She imagined it wasn't something he expressed very often. Most of the time she'd been in his presence, he wore a smile.

Mona had walked around her house placing some bags —with who knew what inside them—around the perimeter. Under the windows, by the doors. Any place that had a means to enter or escape the house. At every place, she chanted a spell, sprinkled what looked like water, then moved on to the next area. She currently stood near the front door, ending her protection spell there.

"Ummm...Charly..." Jock's eyes rounded. "You might want to come here."

The sudden panic in his eyes had her jumping up from the couch, nearly splashing some of the coffee on her hand.

"Mona!"

Mona jerked at the sound of her voice, pausing in her action, and looked at her. "Yes?"

Charly didn't think she had to spell it out to her why she screamed her name, but apparently, she did.

"Please tell me you're not about to throw a whole bucket of water at my front door."

The bucket Mona held looked filled to the top and a bit heavy, if the muscles in her arms were an indication. Which Charly would say was a highly accurate analysis. Mona had toned arms. They were being put to use at the moment.

"Think of the water like holy water. It's blessed. But more like with a spell full of protection. Anything the water touches will be protected even more than me whispering some words."

Okay. That all made perfect sense. It did. But...

"And the massive water mess it will make once you throw it at the door. What about that?"

Mona gave a half-shrug, averting her gaze. "Not all spells are spotless."

"Are you insinuating I can't clean up the mess once you throw it?"

"Well,"—she bit her bottom lip—"it will reduce some of the power of the spell if you do."

"I didn't follow you around the house while you did this around the windows and such. I'm thinking I should've. Did you throw a whole bucket at all those?"

Mona scoffed as if she had said something so ridiculous. "Of course not, silly. I only sprinkled it around the windows. They're smaller and don't require as much. But this is a door. The front door. You need as much protection as you can get. I'll have to do the same thing to the sliding door as well."

Charly had nice hardwood floors. She couldn't imagine that throwing water—and leaving the mess!—would be good for her floors.

But she also didn't want to die. She'd found...well, saying love was too soon. But she'd found a man who overlooked her oddness and wanted to get to know her. Wanted to be in her life. If this crazy protection spell could make a life-or-death difference, then who was she to argue?

"What is the probability of this spell working? Of keeping this madman out of my house?"

Mona sighed, her arms wobbling. No doubt because the heavy-ass bucket was getting to be too much. "I'd like to say one hundred percent. But you know me, Charly. I am new at this witch business. If it makes you feel better, I've used it before and the evil entity I'm keeping locked up hasn't escaped." She lost the battle. The bucket plopped to the floor, some of the water spilling over the brim.

"I'm sure you're not a fan of me."

Charly opened her mouth to dispute that but stopped when Mona held up a hand to let her continue.

"This whole mess is my fault. Because I failed to close the portal. Because I did something wrong. It eats at me every day. Now knowing Thomas escaped and has his eyes set on you..." Mona blew out a harried breath. "I don't know how to say I'm sorry. I don't know what to do other than my best to keep you safe. I can't say how effective this will be, but please give me the chance. When this is all over, I'll replace your floor wherever it might've gotten damaged myself. I promise."

She had never blamed Mona for any of this. She wasn't going to start now, even with Mona pointing at herself as the one at fault.

"I trust you, Mona. I'm not happy with the thought of all that water on my floor. But I trust you."

"Good." An empathic smile graced her face. "And thank you." Then she pulled out a piece of licorice, chomping a large portion of it off. "Oh, and this spell should keep most supernatural beings out. I went with the most powerful one

I could find in my mother's journal." Mona paused. "That includes Donnie and the boys. They won't be able to get inside the house. Once I leave, I'm not even sure I'll be able to get back in."

So, Charly was on her own. Besides Breck and his brother Jock. Well, Kade didn't have any paranormal abilities, though he could see ghosts. Did that make him supernatural of some kind? And Bailey, if she got released from the hospital before Friday, would she even be able to enter? She was a former ghost. As was Mason.

And what about herself?

As a psychic?

"Mona, will I be able to get back in my house?"

A tiny giggle erupted from Mona's lips, turning into boisterous laughter. "Oh my gosh! I have no idea."

Jock cleared his throat, making Mona lessen her laughter but not completely. "Then perhaps you shouldn't do it."

Mona shook her head. "No, it has to be done. Charly shouldn't step outside the house at all. For any reason until Friday passes. Because even if she'd stay somewhere else, I should put the protection spell wherever she is. She has to be protected at all costs."

Charly thought of all the work she had to do in the shed. Of the bench she'd only gotten a quarter of the way finished. She'd be stuck in the house until Saturday. Most of the time that wouldn't bother her because she was a homebody more than anything. But to not be able to step outside for any reason sounded like a nightmare.

Again, better than being dead.

"I won't leave the house."

Mona nodded, and before anyone could argue, she picked up the bucket and chucked the water at the door.

Water sprayed everywhere, raining down on the door and spilling across the floor. The puddle was so large, it caused Mona to rush out of the way so it didn't touch her feet.

It trailed halfway down her hallway and crawled a little bit into her living room, stopping when it hit her rug.

"Geez, and you're doing that in the kitchen too?" Jock asked, his eyes round and filled with concern as he stared at the huge mess.

"It has to be done," Mona responded with such a desolate tone but with a damn smile on her face.

Charly had no idea how she managed to speak in such a way with the cheeriness just on the barrier of her features. Why was she smiling? Nothing was funny about this. Her poor floor. Her beautiful rug!

"On to the kitchen." This time the peppiness of her voice showed through as Mona jaunted—merrily!—around the water mess and toward the kitchen.

"This is the strangest day I've ever had," Jock muttered.

"Me too."

Charly grinned when he looked at her incredulously. "Hey, I've never had a witch throw water all over my stuff before. This is strange even for me."

That had Jock chuckling and bringing back that handsome smile of his.

"I can't wait for Breck to get back. He's going to *love* this new development."

She knew Jock was being sarcastic. Because Breck would hate what Mona had done. If he'd been here, he would've stopped her.

Part of her wished she had herself.

But then flashes of her death punctured her mind and she wiped any sort of wish from her thoughts.

15

He had a smile pasted on his face, but it didn't help the anxiety coursing through his body. The smile fled as soon as Mrs. Johnson, the owner of the stolen car, closed the door.

The entire interview had been unhelpful. No cameras on the permitter of her property, so no visual of the actual theft of the vehicle from the driveway.

She reported it stolen in the morning when she went to leave for work. Needless to say, her day didn't start well. Someone, in the middle of the night—most likely Nathan—waltzed into her neighborhood, picked her car as the winner, and drove off without drawing attention.

To be thorough, he interviewed some of her neighbors. He took one side of the road, while Mason handled the other. No one had any useful information. Not a peep was heard. No one happened to look outside at the exact time the vehicle drove away. Worst of all, none of them had any cameras around the perimeter of their house. How aggravating! He figured that would be a more common thing these days, having security cameras for an extra measure of safety.

He had a system that surveyed his driveway and front walkway.

They convened outside his car.

"Well, hopefully, the crime scene crew will pick up something good."

Holstrom frowned at Mason's optimism. "They could find something, but it usually takes a few days to get the results. By then, it won't matter." He blew out a breath, turning around to avoid Mason's sympathetic view. He didn't want his damn sympathy!

He heard Mason let out a heavy sigh. Holstrom didn't care how much he was aggravating the man. His concern had more to do with righting his girlfriend's wrong more than anything else. They didn't care about Charly as much as he did.

Well, that was probably not true. They had been friends with Charly a lot longer than he had, but it didn't matter now. He cared more for her than them. He knew it! His heart said...

Said too many things that he didn't want to explore right now.

He swiveled back toward Mason. "I'm going back to the precinct to work on some stuff. We're done for the day."

By the tightness of Mason's lips, he could tell Mason wanted to argue with that. Whatever. He wasn't about to take any answer other than goodbye!

Mason must've known he was in a losing battle because he nodded in agreement and went his own way.

Holstrom drove back to the precinct like he said he would, but he didn't accomplish much at his desk. His mind was too preoccupied with too many things to be able to focus. After fifteen minutes of staring into space, he left.

The drive to Charly's didn't take as long as it normally

did because his foot was a little heavy on the gas. He knocked on the door after nearly opening it like he had a right to walk in. He didn't think Charly would argue the fact, but he didn't want to push the boundaries too far with her and she booted him out.

Jock answered the door, his expression filled with irritation rather than his usual happy-go-lucky smile. "You left some information out this morning. We will have to talk about that at some point. Watch your step." He pointed to where a puddle of water lingered on the mahogany wood floor.

"Why is the floor wet?"

Jock laughed. "It's a great story."

He attempted to step around the mess as best as he could, confused as to why no one had wiped it up. "Here's a bright idea. Grab a towel and clean it."

Jock slapped him on the shoulder. "I wish I could. We were told not to. Charly's in the kitchen making cookies."

Holstrom removed his shoes, sidestepping the water, and ventured down the hallway, his nose following the delicious aroma.

Charly's delectable ass was in the air in front of the oven, and it took a lot more energy than he cared to admit not to slide up behind her and pull her close. Of course, he couldn't do those kinds of things with his brother in the house.

His mouth opened to call out a greeting when he paused, eyeing more water in front of the sliding door.

Charly turned around, shrieking. "Breck! You're home."

Yes, he was home.

He could get used to hearing that simple phrase more often coming from her. Strange. Because when he was with

Danielle, he couldn't even fathom living with her. He had liked his space.

"Why is there water all over the floor?"

She walked toward the island counter, setting the hot pan of white macadamia nut cookies on the potholders.

"Mona stopped by. She put a protection spell on the house."

He didn't like the sound of that. That crazy woman needed to stay far away from Charly!

"That does not explain the water."

He decided that voicing his opinion on the Mona issue wouldn't get him anywhere but farther away from Charly. She liked them—Mona and Mason.

"It's part of the spell."

He nodded like that made sense. None of it made sense!

"And we're not wiping it up because..."

She smiled and like an invisible rope was pulling her to him, she headed his way, stepping into his arms. Her soft hand brushed his roughened cheek, then smoothed a path upward until it slid through his hair. He closed his eyes a moment, relishing in her delicate touch. As if she had to level out the anxiety coursing through him. It wasn't far off the mark. His chaotic nerves had ratcheted up the moment she uttered the word Mona. Her sweet touch was reducing it the longer they stood together wrapped in each other's arms.

"If Mona says I should leave the water, I'm not touching it. I'm just as concerned as you about it, but I much rather live to see another day than die a horrible, gruesome death."

His eyes snapped open. "You are not dying on my watch."

And damn it! If the crazy witch thought a protection spell would add another layer of defense, then he couldn't argue with the logic. Not that he appreciated the huge water mess.

"What else did she do?"

"Said some weird spell, put a bag of—" Charly shook her head as if she didn't know—and didn't want to know—what was in it. "Of something by all the windows and doors. Then she threw a whole bucket of water at both doors. Thankfully, she only sprinkled water around the windows. She said it should keep any supernatural force out."

"Any supernatural force?"

"Yes. Which includes Donnie and the other guys. Even Mona herself. She stepped outside and tried to re-enter, and a weird force field knocked her back. Jock had to run outside to make sure she was okay. It literally knocked her off the porch."

Despite hating the woman, Breck didn't want her to get hurt. Especially when she was only trying to keep Charly safe.

"And is she okay?"

Charly nodded, running another tender hand through his hair. "A bit shaken because she hadn't expected such a big hit like that from it. She's fine. She doesn't think Mason or Bailey can come inside either." She leaned closer, her mouth inches from his. "Being they're former ghosts and all."

Of course. How could he forget something as ridiculous as that?

He broke the distance, kissing her until a low, sweet moan filtered out of her lips. Knowing his brother was in the house—Jock had been smart enough not to follow him to the kitchen—he couldn't take the heat building between them any further than a simple kiss.

"So it should keep out Nathan, who is possessed by a spirit?"

Charly jumped in his arms, her lips curling into the first big, beautiful smile of the day. Her enthusiasm was almost contagious. "Exactly. Which is why I can't complain too much about the water mess. Nothing evil can enter." Then her expression fell. "It also means I shouldn't leave the house because I might not be able to re-enter myself."

He wouldn't argue with that. Whatever kept her safe.

"How was your day?"

She cupped his cheeks when he didn't say anything. What could he say? He had gotten nowhere closer to finding Nathan.

"It's okay, Breck. You're doing the best you can."

That's what he loved about Charly. She knew without needing him to respond how he felt, how his day went.

Unlike Danielle who would get irritated that he never talked to her. Never burdened her with his problems, the bad days he would have. The horrors he would see on the job.

Of course, Charly was also psychic, and the moment she touched him, she'd seen everything he'd done earlier. For the first time, it didn't bother him. Not even an ounce of discomfort hit him. Because not having to voice his frustration was a blessing. To know that she just knew helped more than he could express. He also appreciated that she gave the appearance as if she didn't know how his day went, even though she did. It had been thoughtful of her to ask.

"I love you."

She jerked.

His hands tightened on her waist so she couldn't escape.

Why try to deny his feelings anymore? Even to himself. He loved Charly. With his entire being.

If he didn't tell her now, she'd know it soon anyway. She'd see it by touching him and sensing, or reading, or whatever she did when she touched things.

"Breck... you..."

"Don't say I don't know what I'm talking about or that I can't possibly feel that way so soon. I know it's true because I've never felt this way before. I can't hide it from you, so I'm telling you before you see it first. I love you, Charly."

Her eyes gathered with water, though no tears strolled down. Not yet anyway. Her bottom lip bent and twisted as her teeth attacked it.

Those nerves from before were coming back. With a vengeance.

Was she struggling with her emotions because she loved him in return?

Or because she didn't?

HE LOVED HER? It wasn't possible. They barely knew each other. And yet, she knew he wasn't lying. That what he felt was true. He wouldn't have said it otherwise.

"You don't have to say it back. That's not why I told you."

Then why did he express it? If she died—which was a strong possibility—on Friday, then he'd be left with a broken heart. He shouldn't love her.

"Do I get a cookie now?"

For the first time, she was the silent one. Not using her words when she should say something to his confession. Except she didn't know what to say.

She slid out of his embrace, inhaling a bout of strength, then smiled. "Yes, of course. They're very hot. As you know, I just pulled them out of the oven."

Grabbing the spatula first, she removed each cookie from the pan, placing them on her wire rack to cool off. Breck didn't hesitate to grab one, moaning in delight, telling her that he loved the cookie.

There was the dratted word again.

No!

He *enjoyed* the cookie. Not loved it.

"My brother wasn't too annoying, I hope."

Charly's smile widened.

The man himself walked into the kitchen at that moment, laughing. He slapped a hand to Breck's shoulder. "I am never annoying. I am an absolute delight to be around, thank you very much."

Breck rolled his eyes, but the laughter was also sparkling in the depths. "That is debatable."

Jock snatched a cookie, grinning and shaking it. "You have magic in your hands. Do I get to take some home?"

"Of course." Charly giggled as she prepped another pan to pop into the oven.

She appreciated Jock's bubbliness and Breck not pushing the love issue with her. Had Jock heard any of the conversation? She hoped not. How embarrassing.

"Can we not talk about magic?" Breck grumbled, shoving the rest of the cookie into his mouth.

A silly grin punctured Jock's lips. "Oh, no, dear brother, that's exactly what we need to talk about. Witches, vampires, psychics." Jock paused. "Ghosts. I mean, a little warning would've been nice." Jock held up his hand, pinching two fingers together. "A teeny tiny warning."

Breck broke out in laughter. "And would've you believed me, oh wise one?"

Jock tossed his head back and forth as if contemplating that question deeply. "Probably not."

The brothers laughed, and Charly's heart swelled with joy at the sight. Being an only child had been lonely growing up. Even worse had been receiving no affection from her parents in fear of what she'd see.

She didn't get moments like this very often. If at all.

Breck took another cookie, perhaps sensing her mood change. Going from joy to sadness in a split second. They shared a look, the kindness in his eyes telling her that he'd love to give her more moments like this.

That damn L word again.

She averted her gaze, then picked up the pan and strode to the oven with confident steps, even though she could feel her entire body vibrating with nervous energy.

"I'm assuming no progress on the killer front?"

Jock's question told Charly he hadn't heard all of her and Breck's conversation at least. Of course, he had to hear the most embarrassing moment of it all.

"No."

Oh, her Breck. A man of few words.

Her hand tightened on the oven handle after she closed it.

Her Breck?

Was he hers?

Well, he could be. Confessing love was a step in that direction.

She flinched when a loud ring tore through the room. Breck's voice was soft but curt to whoever he was speaking to. She knew as soon as it ended, it hadn't been good news.

The guilt in his eyes confirmed it.

"I have to go."

He had nothing to feel guilty for. Not even leaving.

"There's been another murder."

She wrapped her arms around herself, shivering. Not

from any sort of coldness, but from the brutal reminder that a madman still roamed the city hurting women. Taking a life away without thought or compunction.

"I'll be fine. It's okay, Breck."

She knew no amount of reassurance would actually reassure him.

"Yeah, we'll be fine. Charly tells me she's crazy good at checkers. I'm about to school her at it."

Oh, these Holstrom men. One stern and standoffish, yet warm and inviting when he chose to give his affections. The other cheery and friendly, knowing how to defuse a situation on the brink of desolation.

Breck managed a short grin toward his brother. "Never underestimate her. It will be your undoing."

Then Breck closed the distance between them with three long strides, pulling her into his arms.

"Because I underestimated you. And now you're my undoing."

"Oh, Breck—"

He kissed her before she could finish her sentence. Not that she knew how she had planned to finish it.

"Don't wait up for me. It'll be a long night."

He didn't need to explain why. One, he had a crime scene to assess. Two, a killer to find.

Breck stole another kiss and then left without another word to either one of them.

"I'm going to gain at least five pounds eating all these cookies."

She tore her gaze away from the hallway where Breck had disappeared and looked at Jock. The man had the body of a warrior. His arms were like bricks, his muscles bulging without him even flexing. She could only imagine what his chest looked like underneath his shirt. As a fireman, she understood why he was so toned. She could even appreciate it as a woman because what woman didn't like to gawk at a fine-looking man.

Of course, that didn't mean Breck wasn't toned perfectly in his own way. Not as muscular as his brother, but he still had a body that she drooled over. One she wanted to drool over at this very moment. It would be better than him going to the crime scene of a brutally murdered woman.

"I said something wrong."

She shook her head, wiping away her wandering thoughts.

"No, I...my mind is everywhere right now. You're wonderful, Jock. Truly."

"This is normally where I'd jest and say I know." He even cracked a smile, but the happiness didn't shine in his eyes as it usually did. "I know it's not easy right now. Not with your...vision. With Breck leaving for another murder. He's one of the best at his job. You know how I know this? Because he works too damn much. I don't see him very often. I think the last time was three months ago. But I get it. He enjoys his job. I can say the same about mine."

"I don't understand the point you're trying to make."

She knew everything Jock said was true. She would never begrudge Breck for leaving to do his job, even if it wasn't related to her current issue.

"I wasn't eavesdropping."

Oh damn. He had heard Breck's confession.

"I just...happened to hear Breck...say something I've never heard him say to another woman."

She didn't respond because she didn't know how to. Hell, Jock heard. She hadn't even been able to find the words to respond to Breck. There would be no finding words in this moment either.

"I'm not trying to talk you into anything. I don't even know you that well enough to push you toward my brother. But I will pose some thought-provoking questions, if you will. Because you strike me as a woman who knows what she wants when she wants it."

Her heart hammered, afraid to hear anything else.

"Are you afraid of dying and leaving Breck in a tattered mess? Or are you afraid of living and putting yourself out there for once?"

Damn Jock.

Damn his thought-provoking questions that she didn't want to answer.

Damn him for producing his adorable smile as he grabbed another cookie and stood up.

"Let's play some checkers. I'm going to kick your ass."

She wandered over to the cookies and nabbed one for herself.

"And I'm going to take you down a peg or two."

16

He didn't paste a fake smile on his face because he knew Mason would see right through it. He didn't like the guy, so why pretend?

"I'm surprised you called."

Holstrom was as well. But he had more than one reason he'd called Mason.

"Your girlfriend threw water all over Charly's house."

Mason had the grace to wince and remove the smug look from his face. "She's only trying to protect her."

"Odd way of doing so. Ruining her floors."

"It'll work." The fierce confidence in Mason's expression boosted Holstrom's hope that it actually would. "She performed the same spell on our basement door to keep her evil aunt locked up. She's yet to escape."

"I'm sorry, what?" Holstrom shook his head then waved his hand for Mason to forget he even said anything. "Come on. We have a crime scene to look at it."

He did *not* want to know about an evil aunt or creature or anything to do with the paranormal world.

A small grin re-emerged on Mason's face, the damn look

irritating him. The man knew it bothered him to hear things like that, which was probably why he'd said it.

They greeted the officer standing by the front door of the house. Holstrom gave Mason a brief rundown of what he knew so far.

The victim, Christy Duncan, was a thirty-three-year-old woman who lived alone. Her sister had found the body.

The living room was filled with artwork on the wall. Abstract paintings that were pleasing to the eye, and he wasn't one to be enthralled by art. They made their way down the hallway and into the bedroom at the end. Christy's naked body was on the bed, a red tie wrapped around her neck.

The coroner, Billy Hampton, had arrived already, examining the body.

Holstrom nodded in greeting to the man, then introduced Mason before asking, "Do you have a time of death yet?"

"Mind you, before I've had a chance to do an official autopsy, I'd say earlier this morning between four and eight o'clock."

The time was rolling toward six o'clock PM. That wasn't a very long time she'd been dead, but enough that Nathan would be on to his next victim. If he was stalking them beforehand. At this point, Holstrom wasn't sure about much.

"Anything different that you can tell from our last victim, Carla?"

Billy shook his head, a morose expression filling his features. "Same as her. Appears to have been raped, and not too gently either." Billy pointed to her neck. "Strangled as before. A different color tie if that makes a difference." Then he pointed to the open closet. "Carla shared an apartment with her boyfriend. His tie was used on her. As you can see,

Christy doesn't appear to have any men's clothing in her closet. So he seems to have brought a tie with him."

That was an interesting observation. Carla's mode of death could've been a moment of opportunity. A tie was available to strangle her. Perhaps Nathan liked that method and brought one with him on the off-chance Christy wouldn't have any.

But did it honestly matter? How would that help to find Nathan, which was what Holstrom needed to do.

They chatted a few more minutes with Billy and observed the body one more time before heading to the dining room where her sister sat, crying.

"I know this is difficult for you, but I have some questions." Holstrom took a seat across from her, while Mason took the seat right next to him.

Her sister, Martha, nodded, wiping a tissue under her nose. "Yes, of course."

"Tell me about your sister. What does she do? Does she have a boyfriend? Those kind of things."

A wisp of a smile punctured Martha's lips. "She loved painting. She attended a prestigious art school on the West Coast and got a degree in Fine Arts, though she had yet to land a job anywhere. Her living room is filled with her artwork. She was good. She planned to try and get one of the local art galleries to display her work."

So a struggling artist.

Carla had a degree in finance, though also hadn't landed a decent job yet. Was there a connection there somewhere?

"And what about a boyfriend? Was she seeing anyone?"

Martha shrugged. "I don't know. We were close as sisters, but the topic of relationships didn't come up a lot. She..." A lame laugh escaped. "She didn't have many objections to men. She loved them and they loved her. I wasn't always happy that she was so free in that way, so we avoided that kind of talk."

"Any problems lately? Did she tell you anything that was bothering her, no matter how small you might think it is?"

"No, not really. Most of her time was devoted to painting."

He could keep questioning her and get nowhere closer to finding Nathan, or he could start canvassing the neighborhood and find a new lead there. No doubt Nathan had stolen another car, and if luck was on his side, he still had it in his possession.

Mason popped in with a few more questions that provided nothing useful other than the name of the art gallery she'd been in contact with. Another place to look for answers he probably wouldn't find. They bid their goodbyes.

They were wheeling Christy's body out of the house when they entered the foyer. They followed. Billy stopped at the bottom of the porch stairs.

"I thought you might want to know after examining the tie some more, there was a name embroidered on the back of it. Thomas Wayne."

A shiver rushed down his spine.

"Thank you, Billy."

The coroner smiled in return, then followed the gurney toward the coroner's vehicle.

"I hate coincidences like that," Holstrom muttered as he walked off the porch. Mason followed.

"The Thomas that murdered Bailey, his last name was Denson. But yes, it is an odd coincidence."

Which meant Nathan, who was possessed by Thomas, had used that tie for a reason. Was it to mock them? Rub it their faces? But how could that be possible? Nathan didn't know that they knew he was possessed. Unless he did somehow.

"You know what else is odd?" Mason asked.

They stared at one another, and it wasn't as if Holstrom could read minds. He wasn't a psychic, not like Charly. Not that she could read minds. But his instincts knew what Mason wanted to say.

"Both victims' names start with a C." Another horrifying shiver touched his spine. "Like Charly's name does."

Mason gave a sharp nod to confirm that was what he had planned to say.

"None of this helps us to find Nathan, though. And that's what we need to do!"

They canvassed the neighborhood. He took one side of the street, while Mason handled the other side. Most people were home. Half of them stood outside gawking at the commotion in front of Christy's house. None were able to provide useful information—again. She lived alone. She had no boyfriend that they were aware of. They didn't see anything out of the ordinary. A few had surveillance cameras, though none that reached the road. Unless Nathan walked up to their porch steps, it wouldn't be helpful to look through any of the videos from earlier this morning.

They decided to head to the art gallery next. A lady with a posh black dress and red hair greeted them with a brilliant smile. It wavered when they introduced themselves. Though she was an utmost professional and never lost the curve of her smile for very long.

"Let me go get the director of the gallery. One moment, please."

A few short minutes later, a man dressed as equally nice as her, appeared from a doorway Holstrom assumed led to the offices.

"Gentlemen, Marie tells me you have some questions about an artist who had contacted our gallery. I'm happy to help you in any way I can. I'm Thomas Wayne and I'm in charge here."

He and Mason shared a look. He figured it would've been a struggle to find the owner of the tie. Boy, he'd been wrong to assume that.

Holstrom decided to go right for the jugular.

"Mr. Wayne, can you tell me why your tie is wrapped around the neck of Christy Duncan? She is dead, by the way."

THE LIGHTS from the clock on her nightstand seemed to glow brighter than usual. Or she was too focused on them.

2:32 AM.

Breck wasn't back yet.

Jock decided to sleep on her small couch, despite her many objections. She had a perfectly good spare room across the hallway from hers. Though he hadn't voiced it, she figured he wanted to be closer to the points of entry into the house to hear any odd sounds.

She hadn't gotten any updates from Breck throughout the day. Of course, she didn't expect him to needlessly call her, but a text here or there would've been nice. The only reason she knew he wouldn't be home for supper was because Jock informed her. Which meant Breck had told his brother instead of her.

Why?

Was it because she hadn't returned the sentiment? She'd never expected that from him, especially to be the first one to say it. He didn't express his emotions much, so to hear he loved her...

It had to be because she didn't say it back.

Of course, mulling it over and over in her head wouldn't help her get to sleep. No matter what she tried, sleep remained elusive. She knew she wouldn't relax until Breck got home. By the looks of it, he had no intention of coming back tonight.

Despite her anxiety of not hearing from Breck and worrying about him in general, she had a lovely day with Jock. They gorged on the cookies and played checkers longer than she had anticipated. She could only imagine Jock was very competitive in school sports as much as he was at checkers. The intensity he wore on his face choosing his next spot on the board. The triumph when he would win. The annoyance at losing. It had been a spirited afternoon at the dining room table. Mix in a few glasses of wine, by the time supper passed, her concerns about Breck had lessened.

Now, lying in her bed, the alcohol wearing off, the time mutinously ticking by, it was attacking her with a vengeance again.

This would be the point where she'd get up, turn the TV on, and relax on the couch. Fall asleep there. Of course, with Jock taking up that residence, she couldn't.

A cup of tea to soothe her nerves would also do the trick.

But that would wake up Jock, who slept not too far from the kitchen.

She could get up and pace back and forth in front of the bed, but the way her luck ran, Jock would hear and come check on her. Then she'd have to explain her agitation, and that was the last thing she wanted to do.

Her entire body froze when the doorknob jiggled. A

glance at her clock said only five minutes had passed while her mind went rampant with too many scenarios. The worse one was where Breck had gotten injured. That's why he hadn't returned. Not because he wanted to avoid her, but because he couldn't, tied up in the hospital. He'd never call her from that place knowing how much energy it took out of her when she had visited Bailey.

Then her thoughts emptied and her body relaxed the second the door swung open and Breck stepped in.

She sat up, not wanting to even pretend she'd been asleep. Light illuminated the room when she flicked the switch to the lamp on her nightstand. Breck looked tired and weary. His eyes were hooded with sadness, his shoulders slumped as if defeated. His hair more rumpled than when he'd left earlier, as if he'd been running his hand through it continuously.

"I didn't mean to wake you," he whispered, shutting the door.

She wrapped her arms around her propped knees, deciding a forced smile wouldn't fool him. He'd confessed he loved her, and yet she felt in unfamiliar territory. She didn't know what to say. She didn't know Breck. They hadn't been in each other's lives long enough for her to truly know him. Sure, seeing his past gave her glimpses at the man, but it didn't give a full breakdown of every little intricate thing about him.

He took off his jacket and slung it across the chair that sat in front of her vanity mirror. "You look as tired as I feel. You weren't sleeping."

He said it as fact, so she felt no need to confirm he was correct. Why was she surprised he'd deduced that? One, he was a detective and trained to notice every little detail. It wasn't hard to decipher she'd been wide awake when he opened the door. Two, he loved her. She didn't doubt his words because it was moments like this that proved those three small words were true. Not that she'd ever accuse Breck of lying.

"I'm glad you're home."

And she was.

Commenting on the lack of sleep would be a useless conversation. Pointing out she'd been unable to close her eyes because she'd been worried about him would reveal her weakness.

Him.

She'd never thought of herself as weak before. Determined. Strong. Awkward. Maybe even selfish at times. But never weak.

But with Breck, all her defenses disappeared. Nothing mattered but him. And what could that be but weakness? Relying on a man. On another human being who would ultimately walk away. Even her parents hadn't been strong enough to love her as she deserved to be loved. Not showing comfort in moments where a simple hug would've made her feel a little bit better.

"Your mind is racing right now." He loosened his tie but didn't remove it. "What's wrong?"

How did he read her so well?

How could he look at her for a moment and know there was turmoil warping her mind?

But did she want to get into everything rapidly going through her head?

No.

"Your brother beat me at checkers more than I liked. I find I don't like to lose to him. He rubs it in."

That garnered a short chuckle from Breck. "He's always

been like that. I'm glad to hear you had a nice day with him."

She nodded but said nothing else. Because all she wanted to say was how? How did he know she had a good day based on that one comment? He couldn't assume, so that meant he'd spoken with Jock. More than her, and for some inexplicable reason it hurt.

Breck gestured between them. "It feels awkward right now. Why? You didn't answer properly when I said something is wrong."

He wanted to do this. Okay, she'd oblige.

She stood up so she felt like she was on an even level with him. Though she still fell short a few inches as he was taller than her. But still, it felt better to be on her feet.

"You didn't text or call. All communication was through Jock, and I feel like it's because I didn't say anything in return to your...your words."

I love you would not come out of her mouth, even in that context.

His brows puckered as if rolling her words through his mind to make sure he said the correct thing. His silence and slow-to-answer trait had never bothered her before. Right now, it did.

"And you're mad at me?"

Oh, so he was finally unsure of himself. Good.

She sighed, shaking her head. "No, I'm not mad." Then she shrugged. "I'm confused. I'm tired." She closed her eyes, shaking her head again. "I'm making an issue out of something that is not an issue." Her eyes shot open. "I've been worried about you! I don't like worrying about someone that..."

That she what?

What description fit there?

She wasn't sure, so she let her words end there. Because putting false ones wouldn't do either one of them any good.

"A few times when I looked at the victim..." Breck started slowly, then swallowed hard. "I saw you instead. Your face was all I could see. I'm nowhere closer to finding Nathan, and I have one full day left before he comes to try and hurt you."

He moved around the bed, stopping short of her reach as if unsure he should get any closer.

"I didn't purposefully not reach out to you. An oversight on my part and I apologize. You've been on my mind all day. There's not a moment I didn't think about you, and honestly, that doesn't happen to me. I'm always focused on what I need to accomplish. Today, it was hard to keep that focus."

"I'm sorry?" The first smile of the night emerged, and it felt good on her.

He matched her tender smile. "You don't have to be sorry about that. I'd like to kiss you, but..." He took a step back. "I don't want you to see what I saw today. It wasn't pretty."

No, death never was.

But she didn't want him pulling away either. Her parents, when they started to drift away, it had started like this. Little instances. Little moments that her young self shouldn't see, so they said. Then it kept getting to be more and more instances, until one day, they didn't try to hug her. To hold her. They stayed away. Her heart broke each and every time, until only a tiny morsel lived inside her.

She couldn't allow Breck to do the same to her. He'd claim he wasn't, but he was. That's exactly what he was doing right now. Pulling away without realizing it.

Her foot twitched, but she stopped herself before she made a full step.

Perhaps it was best.

Not because she didn't want to see the poor woman who'd been murdered. But because she'd be dead in two days, and getting closer to Breck would only hurt him more.

"Maybe you should sleep in the spare room tonight. To be safe." *That you don't touch me. That you don't get closer to me. That you don't fall deeper in love.*

Despite him being the one to point out he shouldn't touch her, he looked crestfallen that she even suggested it. But Breck was a gentleman. He nodded and left the room without another word.

17

THE WONDERFUL AROMA of coffee filled his senses, prompting him to inhale again. Maybe it would give him some energy before he even took a sip.

"Dude, what the hell?"

Holstrom turned away from the coffee pot to see Jock standing in the threshold of the kitchen. His eyes were tiny slits, his hair matted on one side and the other side sticking up like a punk rocker.

"I didn't mean to wake you."

Despite not opening his eyes farther, he managed an epic eye roll as he took a seat at the island counter.

"Really? Because I heard you stomp down the stairs. Open and close the damn cupboards. Turn on the faucet. Hell, I even heard you dump the coffee grounds into the machine."

Holstrom laughed, enjoying the brief moment of happiness for what it was—temporary.

"I forgot how you are *not* a morning person. It's refreshing to know you're not upbeat and peppy twenty-four-seven."

Jock gestured aimlessly at the microwave where the clock glowed a bright white that it was four-thirty in the morning.

"Have you checked the time lately? The sun hasn't even risen yet. Therefore, you shouldn't have risen."

"I couldn't sleep." He turned back toward the coffee pot, not wanting Jock to see the reason why in his eyes.

He'd only gotten to Charly's house less than two hours ago. After the odd—fight?—with her, catching a moment of sleep was useless. He tried. He laid down on the bed and closed his eyes. Nothing but images of dead bodies and the hurt in Charly's eyes punctured his senses. He gave up and decided he might as well start his day. It would be a long one. The last one for him to find Nathan before tomorrow.

"How is it you can't sleep next to a beautiful woman?"

The coffee slowed down, enough for him to pour himself a cup.

"Talk to me, Breck. I hate it when you ignore me."

Well, it wasn't a conversation he wanted to have. Would Jock even understand the turmoil going on inside him? He wasn't even sure he understood it all.

Instead of responding, he grabbed another mug from the cupboard and poured a cup for his brother as well. He set it in front of Jock, taking position against the opposite counter, sipping his hot drink and still not saying a word.

Jock slurped his own, sighing as he set the mug back on the counter.

Silence filled the room.

It wasn't the first time they had a showdown of this sort. Jock wanting to chat and him wanting to ignore...everything. What did talking about problems ever do to solve anything? Actions were much more reliable.

"Did something happen with Charly last night? Or

should I say two hours ago? I know you were exhausted when you got back, but the look in your eyes right now is more haunted than tiredness."

He hadn't wanted to wake up Jock when he came downstairs, so he left the lights off, though obviously he hadn't been as quiet as he thought. He was used to roaming his own house in the dark, and it hadn't taken long to learn the lay of the land in Charly's house. Even in the darkness, Jock could see right through him. See through all the bullshit. All the stuff he tried to hide.

"She asked me to sleep in the spare room."

Jock picked up his mug, slurping again. When he gritted his teeth at the sound, Jock merely smirked and did it again. His brother knew what buttons to push and when to push them. Well, he wasn't going to play his game.

"She was worried all night about you. I don't understand why she'd make you sleep in the other room, especially when she originally offered it to me."

He had no one to blame but himself.

"I might've started it by saying I wanted to kiss her but shouldn't."

Jock frowned, not understanding why he'd say something so idiotic. It had been. He should've closed the distance and soaked up every moment he could with her.

"She can see things when she touches people," he reminded Jock. "The crime scene of the latest victim...that's not something she should see."

"So you're never going to touch her again?" Jock scoffed. "Come on, bro. You let her see everything about you to get to the point where you're at, and I, of all people, know some of that shit wasn't pretty."

He lowered his gaze. "I keep telling her I won't let anyone hurt her."

"And you're a man of your word."

"I'm afraid my word might not be enough this time. I can feel the pressure. This huge weight on my shoulders. I have one more day, and I have no damn clue where to find Nathan. I don't know what to do and I'm—"

His hand wobbled, sloshing some of the coffee over the rim. He jerked at the hot liquid but not enough to put the coffee down. Any movement might bring him over the edge. His legs even felt wobbly. He didn't lose his composure—ever. Starting now would never happen. As long as he stood as still as possible and spoke no further, he wouldn't fall apart.

"It's okay to be scared, Breck. There's nothing wrong admitting to that."

Said the younger brother who never felt the amount of fear he'd had to endure growing up. Their dad's drunken rages. Though he never put his hands on anyone, there had been times when he thought his dad might. He'd been prepared to fight back. To defend his family. Being scared had never been an option when he had to be ready for anything. So pushing down that fear had also made him push down other emotions, creating the standoffish, sometimes rude man he was today. Not that he'd ever say any of that to Jock. That's why he was the older brother. To take that burden. To make sure his brother didn't know that kind of torment.

"Breck..."

He lifted his head to see Charly standing in the threshold of the kitchen. First, he woke up his brother, and now, he'd done the same to Charly. Between the two, he'd rather have Jock on his case than Charly. He couldn't bear to see the disappointment in her eyes that he was failing at the one thing he'd promised her he'd do.

Before he could say anything, not even sure what he'd voice, Charly took long, determined steps and slipped her arms around his waist. He shivered at the touch. Partly from the feeling of contentment when she was in his arms. Partly from the knowledge of what she'd see.

He twisted slightly to put the mug down, then secured her more firmly in his embrace. Jock made eye contact with him, bowing his head that his job was done here. Like he'd conjured Charly somehow to finish the conversation he had never wanted to have in the first place.

"I'm sorry I told you to sleep in the spare room," she whispered against his chest.

"No, I'm sorry I said I shouldn't touch you."

She lifted her head. "Please don't do that again. That's how it started with my parents, and it hurt. It hurt every time I needed a hug and they wouldn't give it to me. We both messed up tonight, but we can put it behind us now."

"How much did you hear with my brother?"

She swiped a tender hand across his cheek. "Enough to know that I don't want you to feel any kind of pressure. It won't be your fault if anything happens."

If she died.

She was wrong.

It would most definitely be all his fault.

"Let's start this night over. Come to bed with me."

But what about what she saw just now? The horrible images that were imprinted on his brain. The disturbing interview with Thomas Wayne. She didn't want to talk about any of that?

Well, neither did he.

She took his hand and guided him back to her bedroom where he proceeded to love her as he should've the moment he returned to her house.

THE ATMOSPHERE WAS different this time when he walked downstairs to start the day. Light music played in the background when he stepped inside the kitchen. Charly's gorgeous frame was swaying to the beat as she cooked something on the stove. The coffee smelled like it had finished its job. And his brother wore a smile as he sat at the counter.

"Eight o'clock. Such a much better time to wake up."

Holstrom rolled his eyes and beelined it for the coffee pot first. He'd taken a shower already, so the next step was fueling up for the day. Though he snatched a kiss from Charly before taking his first sip.

"I should've been up and out the door already."

Charly made a tiny sound that had him rewinding his words in his mind. They weren't meant in malice. His main objective for the day was to find Nathan. To stop his madness before he hurt the woman he loved.

The bacon Charly nearly had finished smelled divine. His stomach took that opportunity to agree and gurgled in earnest.

"A quick bite to eat wouldn't hurt before I leave."

"Then have a seat. It's almost done," Charly said, pointing to the spot open next to Jock.

He listened, not wanting to further upset her. It hadn't been his objective to do so in the first place with the innocent comment about already being gone.

Jock smirked as if knowing he'd messed up and was gearing his way to the doghouse. Sometimes, his brother and his simple expressions could irk him like nothing else.

Charly brought all the food to the counter, setting pans on the potholders, then brought plates and silverware as well. They all grabbed their own helpings. He made sure to take more bacon than eggs and two pieces of toast. He wasn't one to express how he felt. Everyone knew that. But he enjoyed this. A hot cooked meal to start the day. A beautiful woman making it for him, even though she didn't have to. It wasn't something he'd ever demand or even ask of her.

"You're perfect. Thank you."

Charly giggled as she forked some eggs. "You mean the meal is perfect. You're welcome."

He shook his head. "No, I meant what I said. You are perfect. And you didn't have to do this."

"It's nothing. I like cooking."

They both knew it was more than that, but having a serious conversation in front of Jock wasn't on his to-do list.

Then Jock opened his dumb mouth. "So, your plans for the day? Charly knows how it went yesterday, but I don't. Care to get me up to speed?"

Not the kind of talk he wanted to have while eating. What the hell was his brother thinking?

"It's okay, Breck."

Even if it wasn't, Charly would shove her worries aside and pretend it was.

"Well, one of the things we wondered—Mason and I— was about the tie. With Carla, her boyfriend lived with her. Having ties in the house wasn't odd. With Christy, she lived alone. The tie..." He cleared his throat, squeezing the piece of bacon between his fingers. "The tie on her person was embroidered with a name. Thomas Wayne."

"No way!" Jock exclaimed. "The same name as the demon ghost?"

Why did it surprise him that his brother had accepted the paranormal world without pausing over how odd it was? To know that ghosts, spirits, vampires, and who knew what else existed in the world.

"Not quite. The man who's possessing Nathan, his name was Thomas Denson. It is an odd coincidence."

"Did he pick the tie for that reason?" Charly asked. "And if so, how did he get it?"

"We found the owner, Thomas Wayne. He runs an art gallery where Christy had been trying to get her art established there. The man is disgusting." Holstrom shoved a piece of bacon into his mouth, reliving the conversation in his head.

Again, he appreciated how Charly, though knowing the facts, still asked like she didn't.

"He's married with three kids. His wife is beautiful, successful, and puts thought into her gifts. She gave him a set of ties with his name embroidered on them for Father's Day one year. Expensive ties."

"We know he didn't kill Christy, right?" Jock scooped some eggs, placing them onto his toast. "How does his tie get in the hands of Nathan? I mean, clearly, he knew Christy."

"This is the disgusting part. He demands sexual favors in return to display women's art. She's not the first woman he's done this to. Christy had obliged his demands. They had sex last week in her home. Lots of sex as he put it." Holstrom shivered. "Some kinky kind that he hadn't wanted to admit, but we persuaded it was in his best interest to be thorough in his accounts of what happened."

"He left the tie there without realizing it," Jock stated.

His brother hit it spot on.

"So that begs the question, did Nathan know the tie was left there? Did he bring his own just in case? Would he have used something other than a tie?" Jock didn't look at anyone as if asking them the questions. More like he was musing it over on his own.

Then Jock jerked his attention to Charly. "What does the

tie look like that..." He winced. "You know, that is supposed to kill you."

Holstrom already knew the answer to that. So he answered for her. "Black with tiny red hearts."

Jock laughed. "We all know you don't own anything like that."

Despite the grave conversation they were having, he laughed as well. "I do not. You didn't bring any ties with you, so that means no ties are in this house." He looked at Charly. "Right?"

She nodded vigorously. "I don't wear ties."

"I know this doesn't help find Nathan, but does that mean he's bringing his own tie with?" Jock asked.

He shrugged, unable to answer that. Because he had no clue, and Jock was right. The answer wouldn't help him find Nathan.

"So Thomas Wayne, despite being a disgusting pig, was not a great lead." Jock wiped his face after devouring the egg sandwich he'd made.

"No. Not really. We interviewed everyone who worked at the gallery. No one noticed anything odd. No one recognized Nathan, as if he'd been casing the place. Following Christy or something of the sort. I have no idea how he's finding his victims." His gaze sought Charly's, who didn't look up. "How he'll find you."

At that, her eyes met his. "I wish I could help with that. I wish..."

Yeah, he wished for a lot too, it was hard to voice it all.

"I should get going. I told Mason I'd meet him at the precinct. If I don't leave now, I'll be late."

"Don't worry about us. I'm sure I'll beat Charly at a few more games of checkers."

Charly scoffed, laughing. "I will not be defeated today. Not by you."

He knew Charly was in good hands with his brother. It made the thought of leaving her easier.

He shared a look with Jock, not needing to express out loud everything his look said. Keep her safe. Keep her happy. Don't let your guard down.

Then he cleaned up his area, holding hands with Charly as they walked to the front door. She'd taken his hand, and he'd learned his mistake. He'd never keep his distance from her again, no matter what she might see.

"Don't be hard on yourself." She brushed her free hand through his hair. "Have a good day with Mason."

His brow lifted as a sly grin emerged. "With Mason? Highly doubtful. The man irritates me."

"He only irritates you because he's with Mona and you don't like her."

Maybe. But he'd also never been known for working well with others. He had a certain way of doing things and other people got in the way of that. Of course, he could admit, he hadn't had many issues working with Mason. So maybe Charly was right. He didn't like him because of Mona.

"I'll be better at checking in with you today."

Her hand sought his cheek this time, caressing it slowly. "It's okay. Don't worry about me."

"Not a chance."

His mouth came crashing down on hers, kissing her like it'd be the last time. She wrapped herself closer to him, her hand swiping up his cheek, through his hair, and then down his back. The kiss burned brighter the longer it went on. If he didn't put a stop to it now, he'd never leave. And that wouldn't do. Not when he had a killer to find.

"I love you."

Then he extracted himself and was out the door before she even had a chance to reciprocate.

Maybe he didn't want to give her a chance. Because if she didn't return the sentiment, it would break his heart. Better not to know.

Especially if he failed to keep her safe. Knowing she'd never cared for him and then dying? That would break him to the point of no return. He needed a chance—more time —to show her why she should love him.

It was his new mission, besides finding Nathan: to get Charly to love him back. Ironic, how he'd had a woman before love him, and he didn't feel the same. He now fully understood the pain Danielle had felt leaving that night. The crushing sensation that he'd never love her.

So yeah, he didn't want to get to that point. He needed to convince Charly he was a man worthy of loving.

18

—————

"HOW LONG DO you think you're going to stare outside?"

The question startled her out of her musings. She turned around from the sliding door in the kitchen and smiled at Jock.

"I hadn't realized I'd been staring long. I should make us lunch."

Jock held out a hand as she tried to round the counter. "I'll make us lunch. You've been doing so much for me, it's my turn."

"You're doing way more for me than I have for you. You're watching over me. That can't be easy."

Putting one's life in danger for another. She would never ask that of anyone, not even her friends. If it weren't for Breck's insistence, she'd be alone right now and be perfectly content with that.

"I'd do it a hundred times more. You're important to Breck, which makes you important to me. Go relax. I'll holler when I'm done."

She decided it wasn't worth arguing over something so

silly and left the kitchen. She curled her legs up onto the couch and sat there. Her musings from before returned.

How was Breck doing? Working diligently on finding Nathan she was sure. He hadn't checked in yet, and she didn't expect him to. On the hour, every hour updates wouldn't help either of them.

She thought of the poor women murdered by a psychopath. One who would end her demise tomorrow.

Then of the ties, even though they might be insignificant, she felt like it was important. Where would the tie that killed her come from? Why use a tie? Was there meaning behind it? Or did he just get off on torturing and killing women?

Honestly, it wasn't something she should be thinking about.

She pulled her phone out of her sweater pocket and dialed the number she should've yesterday. How thoughtless of her.

Bailey answered after two rings.

"I was thinking about you," Bailey said as a hello. "Happy Halloween! It's my first Halloween as a solid human since being a ghost and I'm stuck in the hospital."

"Oh, Bailey, I wish I could bring you a full bucket of candy. Happy Halloween!" Charly had forgotten all about the holiday. The only thing pressing on her mind was her impending death. But she knew Bailey had been looking forward to it, decorating outside, sprucing up the house to look even more haunted than it already did. She had warned Bailey kids didn't trick-or-treat around their area, and now she was grateful for that. She didn't need a bunch of kids ringing the doorbell on such a stressful day.

"I'm so sorry I didn't check in yesterday. How are you feeling? How's the baby?" What a horrible friend she was.

She didn't even know what Bailey had named her son. When she'd been in the hospital with her, her mind had been filled with worry about Bailey's health, but also in survival mode. Trying to keep everyone's emotions and past experiences away from her.

"We're great. We should be able to leave tomorrow. I'm in some pain, but they say that's normal. Emerson is such a sweet little boy already."

Aww. She loved the name they picked out.

"I'm so happy for you, Bailey. I'm so glad both of you are safe and healthy. I love his name. I can't wait to meet him."

If she didn't die.

"How are you?"

She didn't want to talk about it. Because putting into words how she felt would be impossible. So many emotions swirled through her constantly. They wouldn't settle on anything. Sometimes, she had so much fear she wanted to get sick. Other times she was filled with hope that it could only bring a smile to her face. In between those two strong feelings, she felt worry, anger, sadness, so much ping-ponging that it made her dizzy.

"Charly?"

She forced a smile on her face, even though Bailey couldn't see her. She'd be able to hear the happiness though. The fake delight she would try hard to portray.

"I'm good. Despite everything, I'm good. Breck has a brother. His name is Jock and he's wonderful. Oddly, the exact opposite of Breck."

"So, friendly and nice!"

Charly giggled. "Breck has his moments. He's not all bad."

"Of course not. Because if he makes you happy, then he can't be all bad. I..." Bailey let out a heavy breath. "I never pictured you with someone like him. You are happy, right? You deserve all the happiness in the world."

When she was with Breck, yes, her world was perfect and filled with joy. And when he was absent, those damning emotions that brought her down overshadowed any happiness she felt when he was around.

"He's someone I never expected to find in my life. A lucky accident."

"Oh, I understand that feeling well. That's what Kade is for me."

Charly heard a noise in the background and knew the call would be ending.

"I will call you tomorrow when we get home. We can have supper."

Oh, how she wished that were true.

"Let's make it Saturday. Tomorrow is...a big day. And I shouldn't leave the house." Or be around her and the baby and risk them getting hurt. Not that she'd voice it to Bailey.

"Right, of course. I'll still call you to check in."

Her phone plopped onto the cushion after she said goodbye. More idleness. More time to let her erratic emotions creep back in.

It was going to be a long day.

Despite the turmoil causing havoc on her senses, the day was pleasant. Jock made grilled cheese sandwiches with tomato soup. Delicious. Every single bite. They played more games of checkers, with Jock still winning the majority of them. It made her sour each time. The one bright spot of her day, as small as it was, had been Breck's phone call. He didn't have much to report, failing at every corner to locate Nathan. But hearing his voice had lifted her spirits for a brief moment.

He'd said he'd miss supper and not to wait for him. So

they didn't. She made lasagna and Jock devoured nearly half the pan. Probably a good thing as leftovers wouldn't be good. Not if she died tomorrow.

By the time night rolled around, nearing ten o'clock, she decided she wanted time to herself. It wouldn't be good for her wandering thoughts, but she'd rather fall apart alone than in front of Jock. While she knew Breck would work late, she hadn't expected him to be gone this long.

He didn't argue, as if aware of her inner agitation.

She dug through her drawers, deciding tomorrow morning she'd do some laundry. Her wardrobe was running low on her favorite clothes. She tossed on a pink tank top and black drawstring pants and curled up underneath the blankets.

Reading wouldn't settle her mind, and she doubted she'd be able to focus on the words.

Listening to music might distract her mind, but she didn't feel like any cheery songs, which was her go-to when she was feeling down.

So she sat there. In bed. Under the covers. Staring at her wall. Letting her mind soar to places she shouldn't.

She jumped when her doorbell went off.

The covers flung to the side as she whipped them off. Her bedroom door slammed against the wall she opened it so hard. Her feet pitter-pattered as she raced down the steps.

Jock turned at the sound of her approach, gesturing at the door. "Delivery guy."

She frowned. "This late? I didn't order anything."

He held out his hand, his expression taut and his body ready for action. "Stay there. Be prepared to lock yourself in your room. I'll see what's going on. In fact, you should go back to your bedroom."

"Open the door, Jock."

Her firm voice convinced him she wasn't moving from her spot. Four steps from the bottom of the staircase.

He opened the door to find the delivery person gone. No lights were in the driveway, as if whoever had rung the doorbell had delivered the package and left right away. A small twelve-by-twelve box sat on the doormat. Jock peeked outside, glancing around the porch. Deciding everything looked good, he picked up the box and closed the door, locking it.

"There's no return address on it, but it's addressed to you."

She eyed the box, not wanting to open it. Obviously, she had to.

"Let's see what it is."

Then she finished the last few steps, pasting on a merry smile as if that might hide the terror running through her veins, and waved for Jock to follow her to the kitchen.

She grabbed the largest kitchen knife to slice open the tape. It made her feel better to hold such a large weapon, even though it wasn't necessary.

Jock even chuckled at the picture of her wielding it.

The tape sliced easily. Then she opened the flaps with the end of the knife. She didn't want to touch any part of the box. The knife rattled as she set it on the counter. She slowly peeked inside and staggered back at the contents.

Jock leaned forward, his brows pleating as he stared. "That's a black tie with red hearts on it."

Her heart raced at the implications. Nathan—Thomas—had his eyes set on her. Her impending death would happen. Just as she had predicted it would.

Her gaze zoomed in on her black pants. Then they trailed to the pink tank top she wore.

The clothes she would die in!

How absent-minded of her.

She tore out of the kitchen, Jock's concerned voice trailing after her. She yanked on her dresser drawer, nearly pulling it all the way out. It didn't matter what she put on, she refused to keep on the clothes she currently wore.

Her nails scratched her thigh as she shoved down her pants, switching that pair for a neon-green pair of yoga pants. Not loose. Not black. Nothing close to what she had on in her vision. Then she whipped off her tank top just as Jock stepped into the room.

"Whoa! Okay, my bad," he stammered, turning around and shielding his view.

The fact he saw her top half naked didn't even bother her. He could look all he wanted because it meant she was alive. That she could feel embarrassed if she wanted to.

But she didn't want to make him uncomfortable or upset Breck in any way, so she traded the pink tank top for a yellow T-shirt that had a smiley face plastered on the front.

"I'm dressed."

Jock slowly turned around as if afraid she had lied. His cheeks were dusted red, and he wouldn't quite make eye contact.

"I apologize for walking in. That was very rude of me."

"It's okay, Jock. I understand. I rushed out of the kitchen, and you're worried about me. I had to change." She shivered, wrapping her arms around herself. He finally met her eyes. "What I was wearing...they were the same clothes as my vision."

"Now the tie...." He pulled out his phone. "I'll call Breck. And when I'm done doing that, I'll get rid of the tie."

"Where?"

He shrugged. "I can burn it outside."

Not a bad idea.

"I have a fire pit that is the perfect spot."

A triumphant grin settled on his handsome face. "Great. I love a good bonfire. We can roast marshmallows too."

"Well, I can't exactly come outside with you, but I won't say no to a marshmallow if you bring me one inside."

The situation was serious. Deadly serious. But she appreciated Jock's attempt at lightening the mood.

"I like having a plan. Let's get this done."

Jock turned to leave.

"Wait!" She grabbed her black pants and pink tank top and held them out. "Burn these too. I never want to see them again."

His phone rang as he pulled in front of Mona and Mason's house. He'd planned to head home after a very long day of gaining no ground on finding Nathan when Mona called. In a panic.

Nathan had dropped by their house.

Of course, that had both of them rushing to find out why and to make sure Mona was okay. Mason barely relayed the message to follow him home.

He swiped to answer Jock's call as he opened the car door.

"What's up? I know it's late, but I'll be home as soon as I can. Something big happened."

"Yeah, here, too."

He stopped on the sidewalk leading up to Mason's house, his heart galloping at the tense tone of Jock's voice.

"You better tell me Charly is okay."

"She's fine. She's holding up."

"What the hell happened?" Holstrom glanced at the

dark, dreary house, noting how the front door was hanging by only the top hinge.

Shit.

A lot worse than he anticipated.

"A package was delivered a little bit ago." Jock exhaled loudly, making his heart beat even faster. "There was a black tie with red hearts inside of it."

"Son of a bitch!"

Holstrom swiveled around and stalked back to his car. "I'll be right there."

"Hey, if whatever you're doing is important, then—"

"Nothing is more important than Charly," he snapped. He stopped short of sliding back into his car when Mason shouted at him. "I'll be there soon. You protect her with your life, Jock. Do you hear me?"

"With my life."

The call ended.

"Where the hell are you going?" Mason shouted from the porch.

He'd take two seconds to find out what happened with Mona and then he was gone. He jaunted toward Mason, so he could get a closer look at the door. It would be wise to have all the information. Being a witch, he imagined Mona had protection spells on her house. If Nathan—possessed by Thomas—was able to get inside her house, then it stood to reason he could get inside Charly's as well.

"Jock just called. The bastard delivered a tie—the same one Charly saw in her vision—to her house. I need to be with Charly. What happened?" He jerked a hand at the door.

Mason nodded as if agreeing it was the right thing to leave, then he stared at the door. "Apparently, Nathan, or I should say Thomas, is a lot smarter than we gave him credit for. He used magic to get past the protection spells Mona had placed on the house."

"How?"

Mason gave a half-shrug, his desolate expression saying he wished he had the answers. "Mona's in the kitchen making more protection spells as we speak. I can't get much out of her right now. She's on a mission. I can only assume Thomas found a witch or something. I don't know." Mason groaned, staring at the door again. "Mona wasn't home when it happened. I'm so grateful she wasn't home."

"Then how do we know it was Thomas?"

Mason cocked a brow. "Because I also have a security system in place. She looked at the videos. It was him."

"When did it happen? How long ago?"

"Around six o'clock. She was visiting with Bailey, then went to see Donnie and the boys. She only got home a little bit ago. But according to the video, around six."

"So he's had time to prepare. Why come here?"

"That's a great question. I don't have cameras inside the house, so I don't know what he was doing. The kitchen is a mess." Mason ran a hand down his face as a merciful laugh escaped. "And not by Mona this time. He was looking for something. She hasn't been able to figure out what it was."

"I have to go."

Then he turned around without waiting for Mason to argue. He didn't. But Mason shouted one more thing before he was able to climb into his vehicle.

"Take Bozo with you. I'd say Scatter too, but he's helping Mona in the kitchen. The more protection Charly has, the better."

He stared at the wolf suddenly standing two feet from him. The animal was large. Larger than he assumed most wolves were. His round, beady eyes that looked as black as his fur gave him the shivers.

Yeah, Mason was right. It didn't hurt to have more protection.

He waved a hand for the wolf to get in first, then practically leaped into the car after him and took off.

"Who named you Bozo? It's not a very scary name for such a frightening look you can pull off."

Low growls emanated next to him.

Considering he didn't speak animal, he wasn't sure if Bozo was angry for his comment or agreeing.

He decided it was wise to keep silent the rest of the way.

Less than five minutes away from Charly's, Bozo growled again, then howled so loud in the small confines of the car it made him jerk the wheel.

"What the hell, wolf?"

He glanced at the wolf as if he'd be able to understand him. Bozo bared his teeth, growling.

"I don't know what you're trying to tell me."

Bozo snapped at him. Holstrom jumped, jerking the wheel so much that the car swerved and he almost ran into the ditch. He stopped the car, turned to the big furry creature, and thought about putting a hand on his gun. But if he did that, the wolf might take it as a challenge, and he'd never get it out of its holster in time to shoot the animal.

Plus, Bozo was supposed to be on his side.

It would be super handy to know how to speak wolf right about now.

"I don't know what you're trying to tell me! Charly needs me."

He howled, then oddly enough, it appeared as if he nodded his head back the way they had come.

"You want me to turn around?"

A tiny bark erupted.

"I'll take that as a yes, but why?" He gripped the wheel so hard, his knuckles turned white. Going back would take him farther away from Charly. He was so close to her.

Bozo growled again, and Holstrom took that as a warning not to mess with him. He turned the car around. The damn wolf had the audacity to look a little smug.

He didn't get too far before Bozo yipped loudly. Holstrom slammed on the brakes.

"What! What is it now?"

Bozo looked outside the window, then pawed at it.

It was too dark to see anything. He'd have to get out and investigate. The wolf wasn't going to give him a choice.

He exited the car, letting Bozo out before slamming the door. The flashlight he grabbed from the glovebox lit a tiny path in front of him. Bozo darted down the ditch and out of his eyesight. Then a loud bark echoed in the distance.

"You could've waited for me," he grumbled as he made his way down the ditch, swinging his flashlight back and forth.

Bozo helped him along, growling low until he finally understood why he made him turn around.

Nestled behind a large line of trees was a small white pickup truck.

"What the hell is this doing here?"

Bozo walked up to the truck and pawed at the door.

"Yeah, I know. I was going to investigate. I don't need a damn wolf to tell me what to do."

He stumbled back when Bozo bared his teeth again, snarling low.

"Hey, I'm sorry. I don't always work well with others."

That seemed to appease the furry creature, his dangerous canines disappearing out of view.

Holstrom opened the door, his entire body tensing once again. He reached inside and grabbed the brown, worn journal that he'd seen before.

Mona's journal.

It had been opened to a page with a journal entry that sounded basic and light-hearted. Except the notes in the margin made his insides gurgle with unease.

A cloaking spell? Wonder if it works?

He snatched his phone from his pocket, dialing Mason.

"I know what he took! Mona's journal, because I found it. Please tell me what a cloaking spell is and if it works because her notes aren't positive."

"Oh, shit."

That didn't bode well for him.

Or for Charly.

19

<hr>

"I'll be right back. I promise."

Charly nodded at Jock, appreciating the calm and cool attitude he was displaying, but she knew it was a lie. She could see the fear in his eyes. Just a hint, but enough to know he didn't want to leave her.

"The fire pit is behind the shed. There's gasoline or lighter fluid in the shed if you want to help get the fire going right away."

In other words, do it. She wanted every piece of clothing in his hands to turn to ashes without delay.

"I got this." A wicked grin hit his face. "I am a firefighter. It is kinda my thing."

She laughed, enjoying the short reprieve of happiness. As soon as he took a step toward the sliding glass door, it disappeared. The anxiety returned. The fear grabbed ahold of her gut. She felt like running to the bathroom and getting sick.

"Breck's on his way home too. We won't let this asshole hurt you."

She smiled to ease the worry for him. Nothing would ease her own. "I know that. Be quick and careful."

He nodded, then unlocked the door and stepped outside. She locked it immediately, then crossed her arms as she waited for him to return. Thomas wouldn't be able to get inside, not with the protection spell covering the house, but she already felt a modicum of safety with the door locked.

Seconds ticked by.

Then minutes.

The longer she stood by the door, the more her anxiety increased.

She wished in that moment she could see the fire pit. Having a visual on Jock would've helped the turmoil swimming in her veins.

A glance at the microwave clock said an hour had already passed since she had decided to go to bed. 11:03 glowed brightly. In less than an hour, it would be Friday. The day she died.

No!

She would not think of that. She had to banish those kinds of thoughts from her head. They would do no good, especially at a moment like this.

What was taking him so long? Throw the clothes in the pit, douse it with gasoline, throw a match on it. Easy-peasy. Watch it burst into flames and walk away. Come back to the house. At least ten minutes had to have gone by. It shouldn't have taken ten minutes to do something so simple.

She started pacing in front of the window, her mind conjuring too many scenarios of why it was taking Jock so long.

Then everything went black.

She froze, mid-stride.

The power went out.

No storm going on outside, which meant someone cut the power to her house.

Which meant something happened to Jock, otherwise he would've been back by now.

She twisted toward the sliding door, staring into the dark yard. Not much could be seen. Not even the moon was helping to provide a source of light.

Another glance at the clock told her it was too soon for her vision to start. It hadn't hit midnight yet, which meant it wasn't officially Friday. Yet, this was how the vision started. Her standing in the dark staring outside the sliding glass door.

An odd shuffle sounded behind her.

She turned, her eyes widening.

"Thomas..." she whispered, staring at the man Breck had shown a picture of to her. Nathan, but Thomas possessing him.

How had he gotten inside? Why didn't the protection spell work? Where was Jock? So many questions and not enough answers. She needed answers now! And a lot of help because she knew the outcome of this scenario. Piece by piece.

"I've never met a psychic before. How did it feel to know when you would die? I've never actually asked any of the women I've killed before. I mean, they always knew it would end in death. I never gave the impression I'd let them live. So I'd love to know."

Jock said Breck was on his way. That was nearly forty minutes ago. He had to be close. She could survive this.

She had to!

If any vision could be changed, this was the one she wanted to be a lie.

He snickered, then rushed forward. She wasn't prepared for his sudden movement and had no time to react. He slammed her into the sliding door, her head jamming hard into the window. Just like in her vision. The entire scene played in her head as it played in real life. Which meant she fought back. She would fight back.

She brought her knee up, socking him good in the crotch. He groaned, losing his grip. But it was enough for her to get out of his clutches and grab for the vase of flowers on the counter. Not pink carnations like she'd seen in her vision, but the same red roses she had last week. They were starting to wilt and looked near death.

Like she would be soon.

Unless she kept changing the vision. She never changed the flowers. Another detail flipped.

Swiveling with as much strength as she could, she slammed the vase hard over his head. He grunted and fell to the floor.

Her feet moved swiftly, slapping against the hardwood floor as she raced for the front door. She'd run outside and to her nearest neighbor. Not Bailey as they weren't home yet. Her neighbor about a quarter mile down the road would have to suffice. Maybe she'd even run into Breck driving toward her house.

She made it to the foyer and the opening to the living room when a hard body slammed into her. They toppled to the ground. It felt like she'd fallen into a hole, dirt covering her body, no room to move, no air to breathe. He was so heavy and immovable on top of her. Her face dug into the ground. Blood coated her lip where her teeth had bitten into it as she hit the floor. Her head rang and her right arm seared with intense pain.

"Accept your fate." His hot breath fanned her cheek as he whispered in her ear.

Breck said the vision could change. She had resisted that notion the entire time. But not anymore. Not now. She had to change the outcome. She wasn't ready to die.

She tried wiggling underneath him, but he barely moved off her. He was too strong, and she was definitely too weak.

With her muscles anyway. It didn't mean she couldn't find strength in other places. Reaching out, she grabbed a high heel near the line of shoes she kept in the entryway. Then she swung it to her side, jabbing him hard in the thigh.

He screamed in agony, and she didn't stop to savor the small victory. She stabbed him again until she was able to wiggle out from underneath him. The door less than five feet away wouldn't save her. He'd be up and on her before she could even twist the lock. She had nowhere to go but the living room.

The very place she would die.

But also a place with more weapons.

She scrambled to her feet and went for the twig tree she had by the couch. It was long and black and purely for aesthetics, but it was also very heavy.

She grabbed the top branch when a strong hand grabbed her arm and shoved her into the tree. The branches poked her, one slicing her cheek. Then Thomas pulled her toward him, shoving so hard she fell to the ground, hitting her head against the floor. He was on top of her before she could even blink.

He gripped her hands, pulling them up and over her head, locking her in place.

"You're making this difficult. Why can't you accept what is going to happen? You were right. You will die tonight."

She couldn't!

She had to stall him. Breck had to be close. He just had to be.

"How do you know I had a vision of my death?" The words came out stilted and low, and she hated how weak and frightened she sounded. But her life was on the line, and she would do what she had to to survive.

"I heard you in the hospital. I went there to see Bailey and ended up learning so much." He leaned closer, his hot breath hitting her lips. "When I'm done with you, Bailey will be next. I killed that bitch over a hundred years ago and she should've stayed dead."

Kade would never let that happen.

Though, Breck had vowed the same thing with her and look at the position she was in. Nearing death.

"Now you can lay still and let it happen," he sneered, cackling, "or you can fight me and make it that much more enjoyable."

He liked to work out when he found the time, but this nonstop running wasn't something he was used to. Keeping up with the crazy wolf was damn near impossible. The big, annoying furry creature had to keep stopping and looking behind himself to make sure he was still following him. He was, but only as fast as he could go.

"Explain again why we couldn't use the vehicle!" he hollered at Bozo, who didn't flinch in his stride.

They had been at least two miles away from Charly's

house. This would take forever to run. He didn't even know how long he'd been running. At least a mile? He sure in the hell hoped so. Charly needed him. He could feel it in his gut.

If he hadn't been running, he would've called Jock to check in. Except Bozo had given him no time after he hung up with Mason. Off he went, and he wasted no time following him.

By the time he saw Charly's house in view, his side ached, his legs burned, and he couldn't seem to catch his breath. He stopped by Bozo, who stared at the dark house. His heavy breathing was the only sound to fill the area.

It took him longer than he liked to get to a point where he could speak.

"I hate you."

The wolf looked up at him, and again, that damn smirk.

"Why is the house dark?" He shook his head, then grabbed a leg, bending it behind him to stretch his quads. "Jock called me saying they received a package. They wouldn't have gone to bed. Which means he cut the power. He could already be inside."

If his heart hadn't already been pounding like crazy, it would've started up right then.

Bozo took the first step, and he followed. Thankfully, not in a sprint this time. He trailed behind the wolf, who headed for the front door. He had one of Charly's spare house keys, something he asked for a few days ago. She hadn't hesitated once to give him one. The key felt heavier than normal. No doubt his mind causing havoc on his senses.

Bozo growled low and hunched into a fighting position, as if ready to leap to action. Before inserting the key, he twisted the knob. Just like he feared.

Unlocked.

Charly and Jock wouldn't have left it unlocked.

"He's inside. I feel it. We better not be too late," he whispered, glancing at Bozo standing behind him. Then he shoved the key back into his pocket and opened the door.

"You can scream if you want. I don't mind. The other women couldn't help but scream."

Holstrom drew in a sharp breath and put his back to the wall as he pulled his weapon from its holster. He glanced back at the doorway, frowning at the wolf and why he wasn't stepping over the threshold.

Unless he couldn't.

But how was that possible?

Thomas had made it inside. He could hear the bastard taunting Charly in the living room. But that was a good thing. Because it meant he wasn't too late. She wasn't dead.

Then, out of nowhere, Charly screamed.

He jumped into the entryway of the living room, ready to fire his weapon, and was caught by surprise. Thomas stood waiting for him. He didn't have a chance to do anything before Thomas shoved him until he hit the wall. Thomas's forearm went up and across his throat, cutting off his circulation. He ran two miles without a break and didn't wait too long to catch his breath. The immediate loss of air weakened him more than it would've if he'd been at top strength.

Thomas was fast. With his arm against his throat, his other hand went for his weapon. Not that he loosened his grip, but Thomas made a good effort.

"Two for the price of one today." Thomas snickered as he dug his nails into his hand holding the gun.

It hurt, but he still refused to let go. Instead of fighting him on it, he pulled the trigger. The loud bang in the small confines of the hallway startled Thomas enough that he lessened the grip on his throat. He managed to get free, shoving Thomas away. He raised his gun, but not quick enough. Thomas was already charging again, sending them both to the floor. The gun went flying out of his hand toward the kitchen.

Fists started flying, Thomas hitting him good in the face and him returning with just as much force. They rolled and tumbled around the floor, punch after punch after punch.

After some time fighting, Holstrom managed to get to his feet. Thomas jumped up with quick precision as well. The house was still plunged into darkness, so it was difficult to make out much, but he raced for the kitchen in the direction the gun had gone.

Then he saw it. Under a chair by the table.

He dove for it as Thomas tackled him. He went down hard, Thomas's hands wrapped around his ankle. His fingers grazed the butt of the gun at the same time a sharp pain hit his thigh.

The knife Thomas used to stab him went deep. The ache radiated everywhere and intensified when Thomas pulled it out, then went to stab him again.

His hand found a good grip on the weapon, and he lifted it over his head and pointed as Thomas swept the knife down.

Bang! Bang!

Two shots rang out, then Thomas crumbled to the floor, blood seeping out his chest. Holstrom shoved his body away for extra measure.

He sat up, his hand steady with the weapon, ready for anything. A slight movement. A tiny sound. If the man so much as twitched, he'd plug him a few more times with bullets.

When nothing happened and Thomas lay still for what felt like minutes, Holstrom used the chair to stand up. His leg burned with pain and the icky feeling of blood raining down his leg said he needed to stop the bleeding. If it hit an artery...he was a dead man either way.

He shoved his gun back into its holster and hobbled toward the island counter where a towel lay. His hands shook as he wrapped his leg and tied it as tightly as he could. Then he hobbled toward the living room.

He had heard Charly scream. Thomas had a knife. If she was...

No! He wouldn't think it. She couldn't be dead. He made it in time. He had to have.

The lack of light was pissing him off. Because as soon as he reached the threshold of the living room it was hard to see whether Charly was breathing or not. He slumped to the floor.

Charly's shirt was torn, and her bra cut off. He knew she didn't like wearing bras around the house, but she did when Jock was in residence. He saw a faint sign of blood as if Thomas had used the knife to remove the bra and hadn't been gentle about it. Her pants didn't seem to be down, so he hadn't gotten that far yet. Besides the small cuts on her chest, he didn't see a large amount of blood. Though the tie around her neck wasn't a good sign.

He rushed to untie it from her neck, his fingers wobbly and failing in their job.

"Stay with me, sweetheart. You're okay. You're fine."

She had screamed. Then Thomas attacked him. He didn't have time to strangle her. There hadn't been enough time.

Yet, it had been tied tightly. Minutes had gone by with him fighting with Thomas. She could've died while he fought for his own life. Thomas must've knocked her out so that she didn't loosen it herself.

He finally got the tie loose enough to release the pressure on her neck.

"Charly, sweetheart." He brushed her cheek, aching to bring his hand to her throat and check for a pulse, but too afraid to do so. "Wake up, please. Tell me you're okay."

She didn't make a sound or even flinch.

"Charly!" His voice raised in volume, but his hand still made no effort to move from her cheek.

He failed her. He had promised to keep her safe and he failed. She had insisted from the very beginning her vision would come true. And it had. Sure, parts of it were different, but the end result had been the same.

He bent closer, his eyes welling with tears. "I'm so sorry, Charly. Oh, God, sweetheart, I'm so sorry."

20

HIS MIND FELT WOOZY, no doubt from the knife wound in his thigh. It didn't matter though. Nothing did anymore now that Charly was gone. He hadn't saved her.

His hand went to his weapon when a large crash sounded from the kitchen. *Thomas!*

He jerked it out of its holster and swiveled toward the entryway. Two seconds later, Jock appeared.

"Whoa!" Jock backed up, hands in the air. "It's me, bro. It's me."

His hand fell to his side. "What the hell was that noise?"

Despite the gloomy atmosphere, his brother smirked. "I might've thrown a rock through the sliding glass door because it was locked."

Yeah, that made sense. Anything to get inside and to Charly. He wasn't going to hold that against Jock.

"Is she..."

He didn't want to answer the question Jock couldn't even finish.

"I'm afraid the tie around her neck was too tight while I fought with him."

Jock slumped to the other side of her, pressing his fingers to her neck, something he had been unable to do.

"She has a pulse." Jock clamped a hand onto his shoulder. "She has a pulse, Breck. I already called the cops when I came to. They should be here soon. The damn bastard snuck up behind me and knocked me out. I never saw him coming."

He brushed a hand across her cheek, then grabbed one of her hands, squeezing it. "Wake up, Charly. Let me hear your beautiful voice."

When she didn't respond, he looked at Jock. "What happened?"

"I didn't see him. He came out of nowhere and clocked me on the head. I guess I should be thankful he didn't kill me. I'm sorry I let him get to her."

Right. His brother already mentioned he snuck up on him. It had been a dumb question to ask. "It's not your fault. I imagine he used a cloaking spell so you wouldn't be aware of him."

"You okay?"

He nodded. "He stabbed me in the thigh. It hurts like hell, but I'll be fine. I need Charly to wake up."

"She will, bro. She's a fighter."

The night went by in a blur. Soon after Jock had entered the house, the police arrived. So had an ambulance. Bozo had disappeared and Breck couldn't worry about him. It was best he wasn't around everyone. How would he explain a wolf in their presence? Charly was still out when they loaded her up. He and Jock went with her. He wasn't very happy when he had to leave her side, but he'd been hurt as well.

Thankfully, surgery wasn't necessary, but quite a few stitches were. Jock had a concussion, and while they wanted to monitor him, he declined. Holstrom wasn't leaving, not until Charly did. But he certainly wasn't going to be holed up in a different room. He'd be by her side until she was able to walk out of the hospital on her own accord.

Two hours passed before he was able to join her in the room they'd set her up in. She had a concussion, superficial cuts that didn't require any stitches, and too many bruises around her body that he had a hard time looking at.

But he'd look because it meant she was alive.

And awake.

"Charly!"

He pulled her into his arms before she could speak. Her arms wrapping around him was all he needed.

"They said you were hurt, but wouldn't tell me how badly."

Despite not wanting to, he broke away from her, sitting on the edge of the bed. Needing some contact, he threaded his fingers with hers.

"Just a scrape. Nothing too bad." If one wanted to call a deep stab wound not too bad. But she didn't need to know that. Not right now anyway. Of course, it didn't matter if he didn't voice it, she already knew. The moment he touched her, she knew everything that had occurred.

"I was so afraid you'd never wake up."

"He heard you open the door. That's when he tightened the tie. Then he hit me on the head with the handle of the knife. I don't remember anything after that."

He raised her hand to his lips and pressed a long, hard kiss across the back of it. "I'm so sorry I let this happen. You have no idea how sorry."

Charly smiled as she put her free hand on his hip. "This isn't your fault, Breck. I told you it would happen."

This time he smiled—with a bit of cockiness inter-twined. "And I told you I wouldn't let the vision come true."

"The worst part of it didn't. It's a first for me."

"I'll take a wrong vision any day. If it means you're safe, that you're alive, I will take that wrong vision."

Her eyes closed, and the hand he held felt weak, as if she were losing her strength. He lowered her hand to the bed.

"Get some rest. I'm not leaving your side."

"What happens now?" she asked, though she didn't open her eyes.

That was an open-ended question. It could mean so many things. He decided to focus on the one he thought was the most important.

"You get better and then you come home with me."

That had her opening her eyes.

"Jock broke your sliding glass door. He threw a rock through it to get inside." His crooked grin was meant to lessen the blow of the destruction.

It worked because she half laughed before closing her eyes again.

"It's also a crime scene at the moment. I killed Thomas. Shot him twice. But you know that. You saw it. I'll be on administrative leave until they investigate it. Since I'm not leaving your side, that means you have to come home with me until it's okay to go back to your house."

"Whatever you say, Breck."

Then nothing but her quiet breathing filled the room, and he knew she'd fallen asleep again. The nurse came in at the same time, and he expressed his concern. Of course, the nurse reminded him she had a concussion and she'd been going in and out of it since she arrived at the hospi-tal. She could continue to do so until her symptoms improved. They intended to monitor her for at least twenty-four hours. As long as she continued to wake up when they wanted her to, there was nothing to be alarmed about.

Well, he was alarmed. He didn't like seeing Charly like this.

He pulled up a chair and kept ahold of her hand, closing his eyes while she rested. The nurse woke her up every hour, and Charly thankfully responded every time. Not like it was in the house when she didn't even flinch at the sound of his voice.

Morning appeared and his body told him it'd been a long evening in a chair that he would be glad to burn after this was all over. But he was also grateful for the uncomfortable device because it kept him close to Charly.

Jock had left hours ago, but called, checking on Charly. There wasn't much to report other than the color in her face was looking better and she woke up every time the nurse insisted. The bruises were hard to witness in the light of day. The stark reminder of how close that bastard had come to killing her.

He'd left her side once to use the bathroom, otherwise he didn't move. Not even when the nurse suggested he get a bite to eat in the cafeteria. He didn't plan to eat until Charly could. Nothing would remove him from her side.

Around ten o'clock, Mason, Mona, Kade, and Bailey appeared. Bailey sat in a wheelchair holding their new bundle of joy.

"How is she?" Bailey asked softly. Either because she didn't want to wake Charly or she didn't want to wake the baby.

"Doing okay."

He'd always been a man of few words, and honestly, he didn't know how to answer that. She was physically okay.

She was alive. But the things she endured.... Was she okay? It wouldn't be an easy recovery, especially mentally.

"Mona removed the protective spell from her house. We also fixed the sliding door and cleaned up all the mess. It's ready for Charly whenever she is." Mason moved closer to the bed, Mona by his side. "I'm sorry I didn't go with you. I should've."

Why? His girlfriend had needed him. He sent along Bozo, though he hadn't been much help when they finally got to the house. He hadn't been able to enter.

"How did Thomas get through the barrier when Bozo couldn't?"

Mona looked more subdued than Holstrom had ever seen her. "He found another witch. Made her tell him the spells he'd need to get through the barrier but not disable it completely. He killed her. Donnie and the boys found her. She was a low-level witch like me." Mona shivered. "Like I used to be, anyway."

He frowned. "What does that mean?"

"It means I've decided to stop doing spells and such." Mona turned away from Mason when he tried to comfort her. "Please tell Charly I'll visit her when she feels better and is back at home."

Then Mona left and Mason followed.

Kade pushed Bailey closer to the bed.

"They forgot to tell you they performed a spell on Thomas's—well, Nathan's—body in case his spirit lingered. He won't be able to hurt anyone ever again. He's back in hell where he belongs," Kade said quietly, his frequent glances at Charly telling Holstrom he didn't want to wake her up.

"Good."

Then he returned his gaze to Charly, something he'd

been doing most of the time he'd been in the room. Besides dozing off himself a few times.

His lack of attention should've given those two a clue he didn't want to chat any longer. Not that they'd ever cared what he thought.

They didn't speak for the longest time, but they also didn't leave. He could hear the baby start to make cooing sounds.

"Welcome to the family."

He jerked his attention toward Bailey. "Excuse me?"

She inclined her head toward Charly. "Charly's like a sister to me. Something I've never had. I'm not sure she'd admit I'm like one to her because she does like to keep her distance when she doesn't have to. But if you're going to be in her life, then that means you're a part of my family now too. A big annoying brother. Super annoying." |

He narrowed his eyes, trying to figure out whether she was joking with him or not. She wasn't. Her expression held no laughter. Only serious intent.

He already had two siblings, and he was horrible about keeping in contact with them. As the oldest, he should be better. He sucked as an older brother.

"We're going to have to get used to each other, detective." Bailey smiled as she carefully rocked the baby. "I don't envision Charly shoving you out of her life. With the way you're clinging to her, I don't think you'll be walking away either. So that means, we need to get along. One-worded answers aren't going to suffice."

"Since I've known him, he's not a man of many words," Kade replied before he could.

Kade knew him well, despite the relationship they had.

"Okay then."

Bailey pursed her lips at him using two words instead of one. He could only grin like the devil.

"Emerson is getting antsy, so we'll leave. But tell Charly when she wakes up we'll be by to visit as well."

After they left, he leaned back in the chair, his arm outstretched, his hand still clutched with hers. Minutes passed. Maybe an hour. Time had no meaning since he sat down in the chair.

When he felt pressure on his hand, his eyes popped open. Charly's head was twisted his way, a tiny smile on her face.

"Have you moved from that chair at all?"

"I went to the bathroom once."

"I'll be okay if you want to take a walk. Go home and get a shower."

He sat up and scooted closer to her. "Does that mean I stink?"

Because truth be told, he could. He hadn't changed out of his clothes from last night and he should've. He had blood on his shirt. While the hospital did give him a pair of scrubs to wear in place of the ones ruined from his stab wound, he didn't wash up. His leg still sported dried blood as well.

"It means I won't fall apart if you take time to yourself."

"Maybe you won't fall apart, but I might. I'm not ready to leave your side. I have nowhere else I'd rather be."

"In that case, I'm not ready for you to leave yet. Even though my house is back to normal, I'd rather go to yours."

He blinked, trying to remember when he told her about what Mason had shared. Then it hit him. They were holding hands. She saw everything.

"Fair warning, it's a bachelor pad. It's not anything fancy."

She sat up, chuckling. "Since when have I insisted on fancy?"

He stood up and found a spot on the bed. "You deserve the best. You deserve everything. More than I could ever give you."

She grabbed the front of his shirt, fisting it, as if she wanted to shake some sense into him. "I don't think you realize how perfect you are for me. More than I've ever had from anyone else. That's including my parents who I loved dearly despite some of their faults."

He leaned forward and stopped himself. "Can I kiss you?"

She nodded, tears gathering in her eyes. "You never have to ask me that kind of question. I would love a kiss. I love your touch. I need it."

Then his lips met hers. A soft, tender kiss that told her how much he loved her and how much he'd protect her from any future harm.

EPILOGUE

SHE SET the box down on the bench against the wall and let out a triumphant breath. It had taken a few weeks to get all her stuff moved from her house to Breck's, but it was finally completed. Of course, the first week she did nothing but relax around the house with Breck. Talking about nothing. Talking about their childhoods. Sitting in silence sometimes. It had never been uncomfortable either. She treasured that week because it was something she'd never had before.

After the first week, Breck had been given back his badge and gun, cleared of any wrongdoing. No one had any doubt it wouldn't be classified as a clean shooting. Thomas had been a madman. He'd deserved the fate he'd been dealt.

The past week, without much resistance from her, Breck had taken off work to help her move her belongings.

He hadn't asked if she wanted to move in with him. It had just been known. A feeling. A strong sensation that she belonged in his domain.

With everything that happened in her house, she didn't feel comfortable there anyway. Breck knew that.

"This shed is smaller than your old one," Bailey said, walking inside the new place she'd be working in.

While Bailey was correct in her assessment, that Breck's shed was smaller than the previous one, it would do just fine. All of her tools and equipment fit perfectly. Everywhere she inserted her stuff, it fit as if it had been meant to be there the entire time.

It also helped that Breck didn't own a lot of knick-knacks or stuff in the first place. When he mentioned he lived in a bachelor pad, what he should've said was he lived in a house without much decoration.

"I like the size. It suits me."

Bailey smiled and handed her a bottle of water. "I would have to agree. You've already put your touch on it too."

She had a few paintings hung up on the wall. Little random artwork she'd made out of metal and wood as well. She didn't want the shed to feel like a place she had to work, but also another spot where she could escape and be herself. To make it feel that way, she had to dress it up.

She twisted the bottle before undoing the cap and taking a sip. "I'm sorry, Bailey."

"For what?" she giggled, walking around the room and looking at the items hanging on the walls.

"That I moved away from you."

Bailey must've forgotten that, by handing her the water bottle, she'd see something she wasn't meant to see unless Bailey voiced it. The moment she touched the bottle, all of Bailey's sadness at her departure hit her like a ton of bricks. The conversation she had with Kade about Charly moving away. The tears she shed. The comforting words Kade uttered. All the sorrow Bailey felt seeped deep inside of her.

Bailey swiveled around, forcing her smile to remain. "I miss you already. Being able to pop across the street and chat or vice versa. I get why you moved in with Breck. I do. But I miss you."

"Me moving doesn't end our friendship. Or as you told Breck, our sisterly bond. I've always wanted a sister. I couldn't have asked for a better one."

"I wish I could hug you right now."

"You can." Charley sighed, knowing she wouldn't take the plunge.

Bailey wrapped her arms around her stomach as if to stop herself. "Last time you touched me, you saw my death. I think it's best I don't. But I really want one!" She giggled again.

Charly figured that was her way of laughing off the anguish filling her up.

"Where's Emerson? Is he done eating?"

Because the last time she saw Bailey was when she was feeding him in the living room. Breck had insisted she take a break and chill with Bailey, but she had refused. The faster she got everything in its place, the better she'd feel. Each day, she felt a little stronger from the horrible ordeal she went through. That's what she needed. To move on. To erase the horror. Staying active helped.

"Kade's rocking him to sleep for his nap. Breck mentioned ordering pizza. Are you hungry?"

Well, now that it was presented to her, yeah.

They walked the short distance from the shed to Breck's house—their house. What an odd thing to realize. It would take her a while to get used to the idea. She lived with a man for the first time. Not just any man, but one who loved her for who she was. Odd, complicated parts and all.

Breck's handsome face was the first thing she saw when she walked inside the kitchen. Bailey giggled again, most likely at Breck's undying devotion sparkling in his eyes, and left the room. She didn't even care why. She'd take this moment with him alone. She'd cherish it like she cherished all the other wonderful moments she'd had with him since that fateful night.

He pulled her into his arms, pressing a light kiss to her lips. He'd been keeping the intimacy between them light. Something she appreciated. It would take her a while to get over the violation from Thomas's dirty touch. But she knew Breck would be by her side every step of the way, being patient and kind in his understanding that it had to be on her terms. She would never turn away his touch. She needed it like she needed her next breath. But the memories of Thomas's violation would take time to diminish.

"Can we kick them out? I need to work up to being in their presence in small doses."

Charly laughed, pressing her face to his chest to drown out the loud sound. Then she lifted her head and brushed a hand through his hair. "What happened?"

Even though she knew the conversation he and Kade had while she'd been outside with Bailey, she still liked it when he told her things. She didn't want her gift to be a burden, so pretending at times like this removed that burden part.

His eyes told her he appreciated it as well.

"He started talking about Mona again. Look, I get he's good friends with those two. I don't mind Mason too much, but Mona's weird. And I..." His lips turned down. "I'm not that sad she wants to stop being a witch. Practicing spells and such. If she had never done that spell in Kade's house, then Thomas's spirit would've never escaped and he wouldn't have tried to kill you."

She put a finger to his lips. "Don't say it."

"It's her fault," he mumbled against her finger.

Hearing it only confirmed what her gut had been gurgling as well. Those chain of events all started with one spell. While she'd never say it out loud, at least not in their presence, she agreed. But she didn't want Mona to stop embracing who she was.

They needed people like Mona in the world. To make it a better place. To keep it safe. And to Mona's defense, she was new to being a witch. There would be learning curves to it.

"We're not kicking them out. We're ordering pizza like you suggested."

"Fine. But only because I love you and"—his lips caressed hers—"I'd do anything for you."

"And I love—" Pain ricocheted in her head as a vision hit her.

———

BRECK TIGHTENED his hold on Charly as she collapsed in his arms. Her eyes rolled back as her body went limp. If anyone would walk into the kitchen, they'd see she was unconscious, but he knew better. She was wide awake but focused on whatever was going through her mind.

He wasn't sure what to do. If it was safe to move her. That was one conversation they didn't have, and as soon as she regained her senses, he'd make it the first thing they talked about. Well, maybe the vision first, then the rules about what to do during one.

His gaze jerked to the doorway of the kitchen where Kade appeared.

Kade's hand went for his pocket. "Do I need to call for an ambulance?"

For as long as Kade had known Charly, he'd never seen her have a vision before.

"No. She should regain her senses soon. She's having a vision. I have no idea if I should move her." Though his arms were starting to ache holding what felt like dead weight, he was afraid to move.

Kade's hand slipped out of his pocket, phone free. With tentative steps, he entered the kitchen fully. "It's unnerving looking at her like this. Does it hurt her? I've never asked."

He'd never asked that question either, but he'd guess that it did. Maybe not physically, but it mentally took a toll out of her.

"She'll be fine."

He looked down when a tiny moan erupted from her lips. "Charly, sweetheart." He kissed her forehead when he felt her hands grip his waist. "What did you see?"

She found her footing and straightened her stance. Part of him cringed inside with unease when she backed away from him. Why did she put distance between them?

If she saw another vision of her death, she should know by now that he wasn't going anywhere. He'd fight until the end.

Her hand touched her head as if the vision had caused a headache. Okay, so physical pain was possible. He should've remembered that from the last one she had in the living room of her house. She had never voiced that it caused a headache, but she'd been in pain that time as she was now.

"Do you need some medicine? How much does your head hurt?"

She smiled, waving him off from moving toward the cupboard where he kept such things. "It's okay. I need a moment to center myself." Then she glanced at Kade. "Don't look so terrified, Kade. I'm okay."

"It didn't look okay. Don't scare the shit out of me like that."

Ha! Kade thought he'd been scared. He had no idea how it felt to catch her in his arms and know there was nothing he could do to save her from such torment.

Even though she didn't want any pain medication, he decided he'd give her some water. After pouring water from a pitcher in the fridge into a glass, he handed it to her. She drank it all in one long swallow.

Then she sighed and closed her eyes briefly. When she met his gaze once again, he could see she was back to full form.

"Before you tell me the vision, I need to know how to handle you when one hits. I was afraid to move."

She stepped closer, pressing her hand to his cheek. He appreciated the touch. It had been something he'd needed the moment she stepped away from him. He never wanted her to pull away from him like that again. Not even in moments of panic.

"It is best you don't move me. You did the right thing. My parents carried me to my room one time and the pain when I regained my senses was immense. I had a migraine for three days. Movement increases the discomfort. I barely feel anything right now."

Because he had stood as still as a statue. Thank goodness his instincts kicked in immediately, recognizing that he shouldn't move even an inch.

"As long as I live, I will keep you from any harm. Even when it comes to your visions."

"I know you will. I love you for it." She pressed her lips to his, and he savored the contact as if it would be the last time she ever did so. He also cherished the times when she told him she loved him. He never thought he'd earn her love. He didn't endear himself to people very well.

"Tell me about it. I can handle it."

She laughed, caressing his cheek. "I know you can."

Then she stepped away again and he hated it. Though this time she stayed near him, standing shoulder to shoulder, but turned toward Kade as if she didn't want to keep him out of the conversation.

"There's a missing boy. He's frightened. He's tied up and alone. Somewhere in the woods, in a cabin. It's dark and cold."

"So not about you?" he asked, his gut settling down after churning with unease.

"I rarely have visions about myself. These last few weeks were an anomaly for me."

And he hoped it stayed that way. He'd rather not know their future. It took the joy out of it. Because each new day with her was something special, and he'd treasure each one as if it were his last.

"Paranormal in nature or just a missing boy?" Kade asked.

Good question. Perhaps that's why she included Kade in sharing the vision.

"I can't be positive yet. I sense evil lurking around him, but I can't see what kind."

He took a deep breath, then let it out. He was going to have to do something he did not want to—at all.

"Call Mason, Kade. We have a missing boy to find." Then he turned Charly toward him, brushing his hands down her arms until he found her fingers to link with.

"Let's go through the entire vision piece by piece. We'll figure this out together. We'll find this boy."

The beautiful smile that lit up her face was enough to let

him know that they would find the boy. That from this day forward, they'd work as a team. That they'd tackle any problem together.

"We better get comfortable then. Because you always ask way too many questions."

He lifted her hands, pressing a kiss to each one. "Because it helps me to solve the puzzle."

"Oh, I didn't say it was a bad thing. Come on, Detective Holstrom, let's go solve our first mystery together."

She led the way out of the kitchen toward the living room.

"Actually, it's our second. We're one for one on solving, so I know we'll figure this one out as well."

Charly got comfortable on the couch, and he let go of one of her hands but made sure to keep the other securely in his grasp. Kade made the phone call while Bailey sat in the recliner rocking Emerson.

But his full attention was on the woman he loved. Nothing else mattered or penetrated his senses as he got down to business. Because when it came to solving crimes, he was always laser-focused.

"Let's start at the beginning. What's the first thing you saw?"

For Kade & Bailey's story, check out
Third Time's The Charm
A Haunting Love Novel, #1

He's not running this time...

Kade thought nothing could be worse than when his wife died in a car accident—especially because he'd been behind the wheel. To forget the pain, he moved on. Maybe too quickly. Now he's the prime suspect in the death of his second wife. But they have nothing on him because he didn't kill her.

Buying a house that needs more repairs than it's worth seems like a good escape. When he meets Bailey, despite everything telling him to look away, guard his heart, he can't help but fall under her charm. There's just one problem. She's a ghost. There can't be any harm in loving a ghost, right? Nothing can hurt her, not even him. Except there's another presence in the house. One that terrifies her.

Between contending with a pesky detective determined to peg him for murder, a ghost he's falling in love with, and the mysterious accidents that keep happening to him at work, Kade fears he might be joining Bailey on the other side sooner rather than later.

FOR DONNIE & STELLA'S STORY, CHECK OUT
ONE MISTAKE TOO LATE
A HAUNTING LOVE NOVEL, #3

The predator is about to become the prey...

Detective Stella Waters hunts supernatural killers, moving town to town protecting people from evils they don't know exist. When her latest case points to a vampire killer, she doesn't need co-workers interfering. They wouldn't survive a bloodsucking creature.

Donnie is haunted by nightmares of his dark past. He's accepted he'll always live in permanent darkness, but he refuses to let the deadly impulses control him anymore. When innocent people start dying, he's determined to stop the killer terrorizing his town.

Stella knows Donnie is a vampire, but not the one she's hunting. Despite their mutual distrust, they reluctantly join forces. She plans to move on once the case is closed, but there's an inexplicable pull between them neither can deny. As they close in on their suspect, they discover something far more sinister lurking in the shadows—a force that could destroy them both.

Get a taste of this pulse-pounding paranormal romantic suspense where love bites back and danger lurks in every shadow.

Let's get spooky. But not too spooky! Join Mona & Mason in The Paranormal Chronicles full of mystery, humor, a little bit of creepiness, and a black cat with attitude!

The Doll House

He's a ghost. She's not afraid.

Buying a house without seeing it first might not have been the best plan when Mona decided to run away from her problems. Doors slamming without notice, a dumb cat that won't leave her alone, and a handsome man who only appears when he touches her with a touch so cold, it numbs her to the bone. Yet she never wants him to let go. Life just got more complicated, but she's up for the challenge of solving how Mason became a ghost and helping him to move on, follow the light...or whatever a ghost is supposed to do. Only problem with that, the house has another plan. If she's not careful she could be soon joining Mason on his side.

Witch Way to Turn

A journal full of secrets...

Mona is determined to uncover the truth her mother kept from her, starting with meeting an aunt she never knew she had. But before her aunt will divulge any answers, she needs help vanquishing some nasty vampires. Mission accepted. Not that Mona knows how to kill a vampire, but it can't be too hard, right? A stake to the chest, chop the head off, sprinkle a little garlic and holy water. One of those things should do the trick. But there's more going on than meets the eye. Can she trust the woman she just met but shares blood with? In a world filled with more questions than she has answers, it's hard to know. But one thing Mona does know: she's not about to let anyone tell her what to do or hurt the man she loves.

A Simple Halloween

Nothing is ever what it seems...

It's that time of the year, and Mona gets to have fun with the spooktacular holiday, being a witch and all. She's embraced who she is, so why not enjoy it. A little trouble with some neighborhood teenage bullies gives her the perfect opportunity to stretch her witchy fingers. With some practice, those boys will learn not to pick on her anymore. But all of her devious plans at revenge come to a screeching halt when one of them knocks on her door asking for help finding his cat. Well, asking Mason, who accepts. Fine. They'll help the miscreant, but it doesn't mean she's happy about it. How hard can it be for a witch, former ghost, and some vampires to find a missing cat? Not hard at all because she has a few tricks—and treats—up her sleeve.

0:05...0:04...0:03...0:02...
Bang. Boom.

Isabella Thorn has lived her life with vision after vision, trying to help save people when she can. Of course, not all can be saved. Her latest vision hits her so strong, she's out for hours. Worse, she sees Detective Bo Chapman, the only man to ever capture her heart, shoot her to save other people from the bomb strapped to her chest. Now she must come face-to-face with Bo to warn him what's coming. Something so vicious and brutal, she's not sure she'll survive. He'll need to make a choice: let the bomb blow, or kill her to save everyone else.

NOTE: THIS ROMANTIC SUSPENSE/PSYCHIC SHORT STORY WAS BORN OUT OF MY WEEKLY FLASH FICTION I WRITE. THE FIRST FEW CHAPTERS ARE FROM MY FLASHES. I HOPE YOU ENJOY THIS SHORT THRILLING STORY!

NEXT IS ISAAC AND EVIE'S STORY
CAPTURED LOVE
A PSYCHIC LOVE NOVEL, #2

His goal was to kill by any means necessary. He didn't plan on her.

Isaac Thorn has one mission: kill Dr. Redburn, the man who wants to hurt his sister. It won't be easy, even with his psychic abilities. He needs a flawless plan, and Dr. Redburn's secretary, Evie Hartman, fits perfectly. She can provide him access to anywhere in his lab. All he needs to do is sway her to his side. Easy enough. Except he never imagined she would capture his attention. But it doesn't matter. He has a man to kill, and no one—not even a beautiful woman—will deter him from his mission. Not even if he has to put her in danger to get the result he wants.

NOTE: FOR FULL ENJOYMENT, I RECOMMEND READING EXPLODING LOVE (BOOK I) FIRST. ALTHOUGH, THIS STORY CAN BE READ AS A STANDALONE. THERE IS INSTA-LOVE! BECAUSE I LOVE LOVE. ENJOY!

ABOUT THE AUTHOR

I'm a *USA Today* Bestselling Author that loves to write contemporary romance and romantic suspense novels, although I am partial to romantic suspense. I even dabble in paranormal. Honestly, I love anything that has to do with romance. As long as there's a happy ending, I'm a happy camper. And insta-love...yes, please! I love baseball (Go Twins!) and creating awesome crafts. I graduated with a Bachelor's Degree in Criminal Justice, working in that field for several years before I became a stay-at-home mom. I have a few more amazing stories in the works. If you would like to learn more about me and my books, head to my website by scanning the QR code. Thanks for reading!

Scan me